THE LADY WHO CAME TO STAY

The Lady Who Came to Stay

R. E. SPENCER

With an Introduction by S. T. Joshi

Hippocampus Press

New York

Published by Hippocampus Press
P.O. Box 641, New York, NY 10156.
http://www.hippocampuspress.com

Cover art reprinted from the 1933 Knopf edition.
Cover design and Lovecraft's Library series logo by Barbara Briggs Silbert.
Hippocampus Press logo designed by Anastasia Damianakos.

First Edition
1 3 5 7 9 8 6 4 2

ISBN 978-0-9814888-9-9

To My Mother

Contents

Introduction

R. E. Spencer's *The Lady Who Came to Stay* (1931) must be one of the more obscure Lovecraft associational items. It was cited in a list of "Books to mention in new edition of weird article" (i.e., "Supernatural Horror in Literature") found at the end of Lovecraft's commonplace book, but was one of four items not mentioned when Lovecraft revised his treatise for its incomplete serialisation in the *Fantasy Fan* (1933–35), the other three being James Hogg's *Memoirs of a Justified Sinner*, Algernon Blackwood's "Chemical" (in Cynthia Asquith's *The Ghost Book*), and Barry Pain's "The Undying Thing" (from his collection *Stories in the Dark*).[1] There is no mystery as to why Lovecraft did not discuss *The Lady Who Came to Stay* in his revised essay: although he clearly found the work to his liking, he read it only in December 1933, some months after he had submitted the revised text of "Supernatural Horror in Literature" to Charles W. Hornig of the *Fantasy Fan;* and, moreover, the prospect of Lovecraft's subsequently adding a note about the novel at the appropriate place (toward the end of chapter 8) came to naught when the *Fantasy Fan* failed in February 1935, with the serialisation having proceeded only to the middle of chapter 8. Subsequent efforts to continue the serialisation in another fan magazine proved futile, and the text as revised for the *Fantasy Fan* only appeared in complete form in *The Outsider and Others* (1939).

And yet, Lovecraft was clearly impressed with *The Lady Who Came to Stay* when he borrowed a copy of it from Clark Ashton Smith; as he wrote to August Derleth:

> Pretty damn good! Indeed, it gets about as far as anything of limited imaginative scope—with only the traditional household ghost as spectral furniture—possibly can. The creeping pervasiveness of the atmosphere is a thing of sheer genius, & the realistic characterisation of the ancient gentlewoman is marvellous. I can easily understand your especial fondness for the novel, since so many of your own studies centre around prim, morbid, secluded old

---

1. See my introduction to *The Annotated Supernatural Horror in Literature* (New York: Hippocampus Press, 2000), p. 10.

ladies of just this sort. Has Spencer produced anything since the "Lady"? A man who could write a thing like that must have more in him.[2]

Who was Robin Edgerton Spencer (1896–1956)? He remains largely a mystery man in American literature, and the only substantive information on him derives from a brief autobiographical statement published shortly after *Lady* appeared. In it he states that he was born on December 23, 1896, in Ogden, Utah, the son of a train dispatcher. At the age of thirteen he secured employment as an office boy with the Oregon Short Line Railroad. Becoming fascinated with music, he strove to become a professional violinist, but failed in the attempt. After a brief stint in the Army Medical Corps (1918–19), Spencer became a federal civil servant and worked in the Pacific coast, Bismarck, North Dakota, and Moorhead, Minnesota. Always a voracious reader, Spencer early absorbed the work of Dumas, Dickens, and Poe, and later "stumbled upon novels of Joseph Conrad, Samuel Butler, and George Meredith"; but it was his discovery of Henry James, around 1923, that changed his life. Spencer read through the entire New York Edition of James's novels and tales; in addition, he took courses at George Washington University to continue his exploration of "the mysteries of the craft of fiction."[3] He began *The Lady Who Came to Stay* in 1926, working slowly on it until it was completed in 1929. It was published simultaneously by Alfred A. Knopf and the Book League of America in 1931.

The book was, on the whole, cordially reviewed when it appeared. The anonymous reviewer in the *Saturday Review of Literature* spoke harshly about Spencer's imitation of James—"its manner is nearly the worst conceivable, a confused echo of certain inimitable masters of manner"—but praised the tale itself:

> "The Lady Who Came to Stay" is not imitative in substance, but an original and haunting study of human relations among the several generations of a family hopelessly bound together by the tie of blood. The old house in which the family life centers becomes haunted by a series of ghosts or presences who make it the scene of their prolonged struggle for dominance for evil or good. It is a sort of ghost story on the spiritual and psychological plane, not without its aspects of mere bodily dread and amaze. But the deeper horror lies in its exhibition of a living world be-

2. HPL to August Derleth [December 1933]; *Essential Solitude: The Letters of H. P. Lovecraft and August Derleth,* ed. David E. Schultz and S. T. Joshi (New York: Hippocampus Press, 2008), 2.616.
3. "R. E. Spencer," *Wilson Bulletin for Librarians* 6, No. 4 (December 1931): 262, 320.

sieged and imperiled by the passions and intentions of beings whose bodies long since ceased to inhabit the family home. This is enough to say of the tale as a tale. In sum it is vital enough to make one forget its mannerism; and that is saying much.[4]

Margaret Wallace came to a very different conclusion regarding the novel's style, but was in accord in regard to the overall merits of the story:

> It is an uncommonly powerful and mature story, written in a pliable and polished and remarkably unimitative prose. Neither in form nor material, indeed, is Mr. Spencer's work reminiscent of his models, whoever they may have been. His style, in its lucidity and precision, and in a slightly mannered structure of the sentences, might suggest Henry James, but it moves with a swiftness and direction most certainly not Jamesian. Without doubt, "The Lady Who Came to Stay" is an expression of a new and original and very striking talent.
>
> . . . Even if [the novel] had not been written with consummate skill, and with an individuality which defies classification, it would still not be possible to dismiss "The Lady Who Came to Stay" as simply a "ghost story."[5]

Martha Dodd's review is mixed, but on the whole praiseworthy. Finding some sections of the novel uneven, she states that the first section is the best ("the atmosphere of horror is convincingly and consistently achieved"). She goes on to remark:

> This book is an extraordinary combination of distinction and mediocrity. It has, like the best first novels, a splendid, fresh approach; and like most first novels, unsureness in motive and technique. . . .
>
> The conclusion in connection with the preceding symbolism leaves the impression of the author's own inconclusiveness. That a novel avowedly romantic in trappings and mystical in subject should be definitely powerful in its effect indicates the presence of an unusual talent.[6]

Lovecraft's own comments on the novel are of great interest. His remark about its "limited imaginative scope" is a reference to Spencer's

---

4 [Unsigned], Review of *The Lady Who Came to Stay, Saturday Review of Literature* 8, No. 25 (9 January 1932): 447.
5. Margaret Wallace, "A Drama of Spiritual Antagonisms," *New York Times Book Review* (11 October 1931): 7.
6. Martha Dodd, "The Conflict of Two Wills," *New York Herald Tribune Books* (18 October 1931): 12.

utilisation of the ghost motif in a relatively conventional manner, at least as far as the supernatural manifestations are concerned; like his master, Henry James, the ghosts of Katherine and Phoebe are mere symbols for the competing psychological pressures faced by the living characters as they wrestle with the familial heritage that envelops them. Although Margaret Wallace is correct in pointing out that the novel seems set in a kind of never-never-land ("We do not know any of [the characters], in the sense that we do not know who they are, what they do, where they live, or how much money they have"), the novel appears to suggest a New England locale—perhaps an echo of the intense domestic ghosts of the New Englander Mary E. Wilkins Freeman—and this may have contributed to Lovecraft's appreciation of the tale.

Lovecraft's query as to whether Spencer had written anything else subsequent to *Lady* could have been answered in the affirmative, for in 1933 he published another novel, *The Incompetents*. This, however, is not in any sense a weird work, but instead a family drama also probably influenced by James. Only in 1937 did Spencer publish another novel that might conceivably be considered weird—*Felicita*, in which a writer occupies a house with a bad reputation and produces a novel whose central character, a woman, appears to come to life and fall in love with him. Spencer's last novel—and, apparently, the last work of any kind he published—is *The Death of Mark* (1938), a grim psychological drama dealing with the relations of three characters to a domineering man who has become a cripple.

At this point R. E. Spencer seems to disappear from the public record. Not only did he publish no more work, but he vanishes altogether, and we have no idea where he lived or how he spent the remaining eighteen years of his life. His death is recorded in library catalogues as occurring in 1956, but his obituary was published in no newspapers or magazines that I have come upon. *The Lady Who Came to Stay* remained Spencer's most successful novel, having been translated into French[7] and, in 1941, appearing on Broadway as a play.[8] This dramatisation was, however, slated by prominent drama critic Brooks Atkinson when it opened at the Maxine Elliott Theatre in New York on January 2, 1941: "It is a silly, maudlin piece of willful adolescence that seems especially mal à propos in the modern world."[9]

---

7. *La Maison des ombres,* tr. G. Camille (Paris: Les Editions Rieder, 1934).
8. Kenneth White, *The Lady Who Came to Stay: A Play in Seven Scenes* (New York: Samuel French, 1941).
9. Brooks Atkinson, Review of *The Lady Who Came to Stay* (drama), *New York Times* (3 January 1941): 13.

The novel's relatively conventional supernatural effects, along with Lovecraft's reading it quite late in life, no doubt accounts for its apparent failure to influence Lovecraft's own writing to any significant degree. But as a model for the effective symbolic use of the supernatural for the portrayal of character and the conveyance of a profound message about the lingering influence of familial heritage and tradition, *The Lady Who Came to Stay* has much to teach us; and the fact that it conveys that message with such subtlety of language and cumulative potency of emotion demonstrates that, purely as a reading experience, it deserves resurrection to terrify a new generation of devotees of the weird.

—S. T. Joshi

The Lady Who Came to Stay

Part 1
The Lady who came to stay

At all events, the house appeared big enough; so that if Katherine had wondered whether her sisters-in-law might not have to crowd themselves a little to accommodate her, she could be at ease henceforth on that point at least. It was to be noted too, in the expanse of the wide walled shaded grounds, that Mary should lack neither space nor security for play. These facts had of course to be recognized as fortunate; but beyond mere size and safety, the place held at first notice little, on the whole, to encourage or invite. There hung about it, hardly less sensibly than its visible gloomy solidity, a coldness, a queerness, an austerity. It would have been easy to believe that in this garden bright flowers were forbidden, that the dead brown paint of the house was the only colour it had ever known. The windows were shuttered against the sun; despite the heat the great front door was shut; and looking back, as she waited, over the lawn and walks and trees, Mary's mother might well have guessed that the place knew no children, that Mary should have no playmates.

They were received by two tall grey-clad solemn women, exactly alike, and behind whom hovered another, wizened, painted, and wearing a yellow dress. These were the twins Lucia and Emma, and the youngest sister Milly; Phoebe, the eldest, was not there. It was the first time Katherine had seen any of them; and if she took them in with a keener interest than she betrayed, their answering deliberate scrutiny of her, so far from concealing their interest, expressed with a plainness almost rude a large and critical curiosity. They paid little attention to the child; and in the high cold heavily furnished parlour to which they straightway went, the talk turned at once upon the man whose widow Katherine was and who had been the only brother of her hostesses.

It was an ill-balanced conversation. The sisters, with everything to ask and little to give, proved not mere listeners, but sharp and sceptical inquisitors: they questioned as if this were to be their only opportunity, as if afraid their slight defect of hearing might cheat them, as if anything short of the fullest detail would be too little, and withal at times as if they doubted the answers they got. Katherine told them a good deal about their brother; and when at last their questions turned upon herself she was, to say the least, indulgent. There was little delicacy about them—they wanted everything she had; and even if she did a little coldly or amusedly check them here and there it made no difference. If Lucia had asked the parried question, she and Emma would exchange looks and Emma would ask something else; or if Emma had been silenced, Lucia would begin again. Milly, ignored by her sisters, uttered not a word, but with eyes fixed upon Katherine merely leaned forward from her chair's edge, intently, greedily, listening.

"And what," it finally fell to Lucia to ask, "—before Emerson married you—did you *do?*"

Katherine smiled ever so slightly as she answered—"I had been a musician—a singer."

"A singer! . . . Where did you sing—in theatres?"

"Frequently; and often also in churches."

Lucia turned to Emma—"She's been on the *stage*, Sister!" Then, to Katherine—"Did Emerson approve of that?"

"He didn't object. There were things about the life he enjoyed—the travel—"

"Well! . . . Do you mean you continued in that—that business, running about the country, after you were married?"

"Yes."

Lucia paused. "Emerson never told us. . . . But what did you do with the child?"

"Sometimes she accompanied us; but most of the time she was in school."

"What sort of school, I wonder. . . . What's your religion?"

"Oh, I'm not especially religious. But this little woman"—she smiled down at Mary—"takes me very regularly to church."

"Of course if the child stays here she will go to the public school."

"We haven't decided."

It was Emma's turn. "Do you intend to keep up your singing—for a living?"

Katherine thought a moment. "That's difficult to answer. It's a profession, you know, that requires extremely good nerves and a good deal of very hard work. Of that—of the kind of work that is necessary—I am just now hardly capable."

"Is that because you are sick—really sick with something? Your letter suggested that. Have you had a doctor? You don't look sick!"

Katherine smiled. "Thank you; I look terribly. And my doctors—

three quite famous ones—offered me, a few days ago, the least possible encouragement." The smile faded. "So, you see, I am in trouble—really."

"You're a little vague. Trouble in what way exactly?"

Katherine let them wait a minute, and then, speaking more seriously than she had yet done, met the question: "My case is, simply, that I'm forbidden the work at which I make my living. I wish you would consider it in that light; it will be easier then for you to understand why I have come, why *we* have come. I haven't the least notion of what claims I may have upon you—upon my husband's family . . . but one must have food and shelter. If I have the right—the least right, on any ground—to seek them here, I can't choose but to take advantage of it. Please understand me. I didn't say this in my letter to you, because I was afraid you might *not* understand. But I am trying neither to play upon your sympathies nor to scare you with promises of a lawsuit. I want as little to demand as to beg. It needs only your right recognition to make both unnecessary."

It was all clear, this statement, of the faintest shadow of entreaty, of threat, of extravagance; only towards the last she was perhaps more earnest than she knew—earnest enough at least to betray her own sense of the importance of what she said—and, what was more to her purpose, to leave with her listeners an impression that held them quiet for some seconds after she had finished.

Emma answered her. "Your letter was explicit enough, anyhow, to leave us no doubt of what you expect of us—and I remember you said you felt quite justified about it. With your viewpoint no doubt you do. . . . Well, for Emerson's sake we've decided to adopt your viewpoint. You may suppose that we've had one, quite different, of our own; but that doesn't matter just now—the important thing is that you're to stay. I think you'll be comfortable enough here: nothing will be required of you but decent behaviour and punctuality at meals; the servants will respect your wishes; and of course you'll have full use of the library, the music room, and the other open rooms of the house. The child will have the run of the grounds for exercise—except on Sundays; but she must be quiet indoors. She'll sleep in what used to be the nursery—which adjoins the room you will occupy. . . . If you like," she finished, rising abruptly, "we'll go to your room now."

So it ended. They all arose, and marched in procession to the rooms—the twins leading, Milly trailing softly behind—across the hallway, up the stairs, along a dark stuffy corridor with a half-dozen closed doors on either hand and three descending steps at its far end, and into the nursery. This was large and high, with windows facing east and south; in it stood a great bed, a chest for a child's clothing, shelves for a child's books, a closet for a child's toys, a table for a child's tea—a place indeed to delight a little girl—except that just now it was shuttered and sunless and chilly. They passed into Katherine's room, talked a little about it—the view it offered, how it had been Emerson's, and how, too, Emerson had been the last to use the nursery—and then the sisters went away.

Katherine sank into a chair, and the child, her eyes large with unspoken questions, stood close to her. Katherine encircled her with one arm. Mary whispered—"Well, Mother—?"

"Yes?"

"Are *those* ladies Daddy's sisters?"

I

It turned out that Emma's statement of the terms on which they were to remain had been quite adequate—indeed, their adjustment into the routine of the house proceeded so smoothly as to suggest, simply, that the sisters had anticipated all the differences that process would make, and had arranged to meet them by requiring only those sufficiently simple observances. Not, conceivably, that there had been so very much arranging to do: the routine itself remained too simple ever to have been enlarged from one much more so. Two more places had to be set at the table; Mrs. Stroub the housekeeper had the two extra rooms to look after; the cook had a child's appetite to think about; and the differences appeared to end about there. At half past eight in the morning they all met, as the sisters alone must have done before, at table—all, that is, except Phoebe, who didn't eat breakfast. After breakfast Milly went out somewhere, and the twins, who conducted the business of the house, went about that business. Lunch, except for the menu and the presence of Phoebe, was like breakfast. For a couple of hours in the afternoon the twins sat formally in their parlour. There were few callers—a simpering preacher, one or two old ladies, and a friendly physician who inquired about Phoebe's health. The evenings were passed in the parlour, and Milly, who wouldn't be out after dark, was usually on hand with something to talk about. This was the schedule; it differed on Sundays to permit church attendance, but, in the main, not otherwise.

Among the sisters themselves, however, there was variety enough—except that the twins differed from each other not at all. These ladies had long white faces and protruding pale blue eyes, and they moved about silently, stiff and straight and always together, in grey dresses and long wrinkling soft-leather shoes. They managed at least three times each week to poke their noses into every room and closet—except Phoebe's—in the great old house, and they had a habit of turning up in the most unexpected places—at a turn of the upstairs corridor, behind a library curtain, in one's room when one had been out of it. They were singularly uneasy women, and inordinately curious—not idly, for simple curiosity's sake, but—it was obvious—because they were suspicious. They acted as if they had been so forever. They seemed half miserable most of the time with mistrusts—ridden with an everlasting desire to find someone guilty of something. They suspected the grocer's boy of stealing their apples, the kitchen-maid of lying about a broken tea-cup, the gardener of dispensing their fern-shoots; and they had a way of bringing people to trial. . . . On these occasions they would sit, with the victim between them, and question and question, watching like hawks, in their half-deafness, for their answers, their faces twitching with interest, their big eyes sticking out, their enjoyment running high; and the more difficult the case the better they seemed to like it. These scenes, sometimes ridiculous, sometimes cruel, often lasted a long time—usually until the culprit lost his temper or burst into tears; and then, if it were a man and he roundly swore at them, as did happen occasionally, he would probably be told to leave; and if it were a woman who must at all costs keep her place, a lecture, an apology, and an imposition of extra duty might close the case. Only, noticeably, it was seldom closed without confirmation, true or false, of the twins' suspicions; they seemed to dislike above everything to have been mistaken.

Milly was quite different. She had a curiosity too, but it was of the commoner type—that which sends droves of ladies, on occasion, into court rooms, which interests good women in doubtful women's love affairs. Milly had an odd little painted lipless face with red-rimmed eyes, and greying yellow hair; she wore gaudy clothes and high heels; and the movements of her little body were quick and silent, like those of a small animal. She was full of simpering talk for anyone who would listen to her, and habitually whispered to herself when she had no auditor. She was almost never at home except for meals and after dark; and, except that she attended innumerable weddings, no one ever seemed to know where she went. However, the abundance, and not less the intimate personal quality, of information she brought home suggested that at all events its sources were both varied and numerous. One imagined her gossiping with waitresses, strolling with nurse-girls, tripping into all sorts of houses—exchanging scandal in some steaming kitchen with a washwoman, in the company of draped forms with a dressmaker, over a cup of tea with the minister's wife. And, for a non-participant, she could make an extraordinarily great deal of a wedding. In an evening after she had attended one she would discuss at length the people who were there, the clothes they wore, the apparent states of mind of the bride and her mother and the groom and his mother, and various other things, as long as her sisters would listen; and when they wouldn't, she would go off into a corner, where she could whisper to herself and giggle undisturbed, and whence she might glance frequently at the clock—for she would know the bridal schedule to the last detail. When the more or less horrified twins tried, as they did occasionally, to restrain her imagination, or at least to redirect it according to their own notions of propriety, she laughed at them—though, in spite of her disregard of their advice, it was still plain enough that she feared them a little. Indeed, she seemed a little nervously to fear almost everything—and she was frankly, decidedly, afraid of Phoebe.

There was good reason for this; for Phoebe was a serious matter. She was an unhealthy, gloomy woman, large with puffy fat, and dressed always in dull black. Her face, which seemed heavy—as though the flesh in it weighed too much—was wide and sallow-skinned, and she had a moustache, and two bristling moles on one cheek. She never smiled, sometimes passed days without speaking, and had a violent temper. Not only Milly, but everyone in the house was afraid of her—even, it appeared, the twins. Most of her time was spent in knitting and thinking. The knitting was superb—shawls, jackets, bags, bedspreads, gloves, rich in varied stitches and yarns and colours, designed with a sure artistic skill of half a century's practice—and each piece of it, when done, disappeared into her room not to be seen again. But the thinking, assuredly, had no beauty about it. . . . She had heavy-browed smouldering brown eyes with the whites gone yellow, and during her contemplations they would usually be fixed, for minutes on end and in a manner disquieting to say the least, upon something—or somebody. There was never any knowing what went on behind them; they simply looked, minute after minute, minute after minute, until whoever they were fixed upon got out of sight, or she resumed her knitting, or something unpleasant happened. For not seldom the object of her stare was a source of annoyance to her, and in such a case the object, like as not, would suffer for it. Once at table it happened that she scalded her mouth with tea and then, half a minute later, upset the cup. The sisters stopped eating; Milly went white; the maid sneaked away; Phoebe sat glaring at the overturned cup. When she finally stood up, it was to shatter that and every other dish within reach. All this, as was usual with her, passed without speech. She had a harsh voice, like a man's, whose use might have rounded out such a scene very well; but she didn't use it; she almost never used it. Another time—a firelit evening downstairs—she became absorbed in the dress Milly was wearing—an airy pink and green thing without sleeves and several inches too short. No one noticed the stare until Phoebe was on her feet making straight for her sister; and then it was too late. The twins, who a moment earlier might have intervened, seemed suddenly powerless—standing motionless and staring where they had risen. Milly screamed and leaped up to run; but Phoebe seized her, and before letting go had ripped the dress to the last shred from the shaking, yelling little figure and thrown it into a corner. Then, still silently, she gathered up her knitting and lumbered off to her room. This was her habit—to shut herself up, sometimes for days, after such outbursts. What she did alone in her room nobody knew; the food left on a tray outside her door was sometimes eaten and sometimes not; but the servants and the sisters passed the door on tiptoe.

II

It was not long in becoming evident that to these ladies Katherine would remain, almost as wholly as she had ever been, an outsider. They doubtless didn't know—and quite naturally—what to make of her: they considered her, maybe, a little in awe; they whispered and talked and speculated about her—about the letters that came for her, about her good looks and her red hair, about her "past" as to which they could at best only forever helplessly wonder; but they were obviously a little wary of her. They accepted her, dutifully and coolly, as a person—but always unmistakably as a stranger—with a claim upon their house, who had come there to stay; but clearly they'd never like her. She appeared civilly indifferent about it, returned no sign of her regard for them, and evidently had ideas of her own as to how seriously, on the whole, they were to be taken. Milly failed to irritate her, and she was dismayed neither by the dignity of the twins nor the rages of Phoebe. They might have suspected—and especially the suspicious twins might—that she even despised them a little; but there was no being sure of it. . . . There was no being sure how such a woman felt about anything.

Her beginnings with Milly and Phoebe hadn't been of the best; but if they had spoiled the future for the scanty amity of those ladies, they had also redeemingly spoiled it in some measure for the two kinds of annoyance those ladies were fit to inflict.

Her coming must at first, however, have seemed a godsend to Milly. If the little lady had been genuinely glad, if only for an antidote to her sisters, it would have been natural enough; but in Katherine's particular

case she would hardly have failed to expect far more than the mere relief of a stranger's presence. Here was a woman who had actually been
on the stage—and who must, perforce, be a little wicked—must know
at first hand the world of Milly's lurid novels: the luxury, the freedom,
the swift life, the revels, the quarrels, the love affairs, about which she
had read and dreamed for thirty years. What glories such a person must
have to talk about, what tales to tell! ... And so Milly had begun by
openly admiring, by all but fondling her, had extended a multitude of
accommodations, had let her into the secrets and the haunted crannies
of the old house, had listened entranced as she talked, had gushed and
simpered and angled patiently for a long time—had caught nothing—
and had ended by looking a little ridiculous.

With Phoebe there had been no such waste of time. By what was
manifestly an established custom, Phoebe's wishes were the acknowledged first laws of the house; and perhaps of these the most rigidly observed was this, that nobody should touch or move or molest anything
which was hers—least of all her precious knitting. Katherine was re-
minded of this one afternoon while examining a nearly finished shawl
into which had been worked, by an elaborate complexity of stitches, a
pattern altogether too handsome not to be admired—had been re-
minded simply by looking up into the horrified face of a house-girl who
had observed her handling the shawl. "I don't know what'd happen,
ma'am," whispered the girl, "if she knew you'd touched it. . . ."

That evening—a still dull usual evening—Katherine sat with the
sisters: the fire, which had hardly been necessary, was almost out; the
clock ticked; Milly, in her corner, mumbled and giggled to herself; the
twins discoursed seriously in loud whispers; Katherine was reading;
Phoebe had just sat down to knit. But abruptly—so abruptly that the
difference had almost the distinctness of a sound—the quiet dropped to
silence, and Katherine looked up. The twins and Milly were watching
Phoebe, and Phoebe, whose shawl lay on the floor, was staring at something in her fingers—a shining red-gold hair. Katherine, like the sisters,
watched her; and when, after a time, she raised her eyes, it was to fix
them upon the only head of red hair in the house—Katherine's. There
could have been no doubt in the minds of her watchers as to what was
coming: that look had presaged more violences than one, including the
destruction of the breakfast china, and of Milly's pink and green dress—
and Phoebe's sisters went now a shade paler. Characteristically, her own
eyes didn't waver; slowly, verily by inches, she got out of her chair, took
a step, two steps; and Katherine rose to meet her. This motion shook
the old lady's stare, and their eyes met—met and held for seconds,

while Phoebe's breath came noisily and her lifted hands trembled within a foot of Katherine's head. . . .

"Don't touch me!"—the words dropped slowly—imperious, sharply distinct—and the tension passed. The sisters breathed; Phoebe's arms came slowly to her sides. She turned a queer, puzzled look upon the twins, and then, returning to her shawl, snatched it up, threw it into the fireplace, and went off to her room. The twins, with Milly after them, followed—to help her, perhaps, on the stairs—and Katherine, retrieving and carrying with her the damaged shawl, went upstairs too.

On Phoebe's part, the visible results of this passage were that she didn't reappear for five days, and that from now on she spoke not at all to the guest but stared at her, in a particularly significant way, a good deal oftener. That she chose to be permanently silent counted of course for little, for she had almost never had anything to say to Katherine anyway; but her looks—always now blackly contemplative, portentous of Heaven knew what—seemed a little plainly to hint that it might sometime count for something that she had conceived a hatred for Mary's mother. The twins at any rate clearly thought so—doubtless because they knew how little difference, except for the effect of ripening that hatred, any passage of time would make. So they eyed Phoebe while she stared, and exchanged glances, and made much, in private, of the quarrel, its effects, its possibilities. It had had, moreover, another significance—in just providing, as it did better than anything the sisters had yet seen, a measure of a distance between them and their guest of a sort which no mere dependence would ever bridge. . . . They left her, henceforth, more than ever alone.

She was not, fortunately, restricted to the mercies of their association. Before the progress of her illness prevented, she spent many hours away from the house; the library, which the sisters rarely entered except to inspect, was a veritable treasury of diversion; and she had, always, little Mary. She played a good deal with the child—in the grounds on fine days, in their rooms on bad—and they made an abundance of the only laughter in the house. They spent hours over books and lessons and at the piano; Katherine took her to school and went there to meet her; and regularly on Sundays, early in the morning, Mary took *her*, as she had said, to church. From the windows the twins usually watched them when they went out, and not seldom saw them return, accompanied sometimes by a half-dozen jostling children who chattered at Mary's mother and fought for her hands, who clustered about her, growing sober at the gate, and at last, casting curious glances up at the dark old house, passed on down the street.

And, for Katherine, there was always the mitigating high charm of music. For reasons having doubtless to do with her illness she sang seldom, and then for the most part only already long-practiced much-loved things exacting little and yielding much—always as though, forced to restricted choice, she chose with care, and then tenderly made the loveliest most of her choice. But she played unrestrained at the piano—played cleanly, confidently, nobly, as an artist; at improvisation, themes various as moods, mostly serious, always charming, came to life under her hands; developments, skilful and sure, rich and free in variety of tone and mood, fairly flowed from her fingers—flowed in music that marched, that lingered, that breathed beauty and warmth—that sang abandon—that whispered mysteries. . . .

It was here, at the piano, that, consciously or not, she most escaped her hostesses—seemed least to remember their existence, seemed freest above all of any susceptibility to the things that their dislike for her discovered; and it was when she played, not less, that they—the twins—concentratedly attentive enough at any time, looked at each other oftenest in wonder and listened most intently—listened perhaps a little because it was difficult not to, listened mostly because of the things Katherine's music peculiarly meant—or almost meant—and did. For, in effect, it came nearer than anything else they could know to revealing her—to betraying what she thought—what, simply, in a hundred unfathomable ways, she *was*. It sang and sighed and rippled and thundered suggestions that they were far too perceptive not to catch, however vaguely and futilely, the hint of: somewhere in it were all the things, verily all the things, there were to be known about her. . . . It promised and promised secrets, and it seemed ever on the point—just on the point—of yielding them up.

Its effect upon Milly was quite other: she, so far from waiting for it, from listening to it, clearly and unaffectedly did not like it. Early in their acquaintance, when for a time she had appeared to admire it along with everything else about her sister-in-law, she had one day taken her through the house, telling her as they went an old family tale. It, the tale, had begun just outside a room which, locked against them, they had passed by; and it developed principally about some evidence that an ancestor who for years had used that room and at last died there, had not nevertheless ceased to occupy it. Milly had been, on this point, seriously, half-fearfully explicit: the twins themselves as children, she said, had *seen* him—"afterwards"; and the twins kept sacredly the key to his room, which had not now been used for forty years. Sister Phoebe said it was all superstitious nonsense, and called her sisters fools; but Sister Phoebe was like that. . . .

How little Milly was "like that", how little she was capable of sharing her old sister's scorn, came out on two occasions that day—once only in the expression of her queer little face as they had stopped in the shadowed attic, suddenly, a little strangely, and before the tale was finished, to look into each other's eyes; and again later as she listened to Katherine work out at the piano the compact Schumannesque small structure of what they were henceforth to know as the *Ghost Piece*. Katherine, visibly interestedly pleased with it, shaped it with care, filled it with colour—with the tone and the air of darkness, of soundless motion, of stealthy presences, of stalking shadows; and Milly, unable to ignore its suggestion, sat straight in her chair, with its disquieting, pregnant vividness driving deeper with every phrase into her mind—until at last with a gulp and a shudder she sprang up, clapped her hands over her ears, and ran off to where her sisters were. Henceforth and increasingly distinct her dislike for Katherine's playing showed: she listened to it, if at all, uneasily—as though she were afraid of it. Maybe she was—afraid that in the next minute as she listened the provocative *Ghost Piece* itself would sound again; but more likely, in her susceptible little mind, any passage of notes too explicitly recalled not only the piece but the day and the tale that had inspired it, that moment in the attic, and some old unbearable fear of hidden potential horrors.

Of them all, however, it was upon Phoebe that the music had most pronounced—and strangest—apparent effect. Certainly the old lady had never before heard anything like it, had no way of knowing, and—unlike the twins—no reason for caring, what it was all about; but something in her dark old soul knew, knew finally, knew with a knowledge deeper than any inculcation of experience, that here was beauty. It may—it must—have lain deep indeed, that sense; but it was assuredly abundantly there . . . for, after all, Phoebe too was an artist. But her response, whatever its profundity within, was true outwardly, as everything about her was true, to her changeless, silent, inscrutable self. It reflected no hint of the significance of her recognition—no sign (as in Milly's case) of what the music did for her; it showed only—but more than ever remarkably—as *attention*; simply that staring, intense attention. Her habit—that evidently irresistible need to get as near to, actually to seize if possible, the thing that held her interest—had here a little to go unsatisfied, however; she couldn't lay her strong old hands on sounds, nor stare at them as she did at other things—as though, forever unable sufficiently to envelop them with her thought, she sought to absorb them bodily through her eyes. But she could listen as concentratedly as she could look; and so now she did—standing outside the curtains of the music room, peering between them, blind and deaf to everything else, forgetting for the hour, one might have said, even to hate the woman at the piano. If anyone passed near her she paid no heed; if Katherine paused, she waited; and when the playing was finished, she slowly, reluctantly it appeared, grudgingly even, went away. It seemed to make no difference what the mood of the music was—but there were times when the curtains trembled in her grasp, and sometimes she stood unmoving for minutes on end after the sound had stopped. If Katherine knew, she didn't acknowledge it; but on two occasions she had been not a little startled in facing about to find that her auditress had not stopped outside the curtains but had come silently in and was standing there, huge and dark, just behind her, watching—watching as only Phoebe could. . . .

III

But the time came at last when Phoebe ceased to be fascinated, Milly to be threatened, the twins to be mystified—because the music ceased to sound. Katherine's illness grew steadily worse; so that, over a passage of months, her absences from the house, her walks with Mary, their play in the grounds, became less and less frequent and finally stopped. She began to miss meals; passages came of days together when she kept to her room; and her chair in the library was at last permanently vacant. The sisters seemed now no longer to doubt the fact of her illness; but they showed for it, as yet, no great concern—seemed even to draw from it a kind of satisfaction. It gave them something to talk about—another source of conjecture about her; and, since it kept her so much to herself, it helped to a restoration of the domestic order of the time before she had come. The twins and Milly went about their businesses as before; Phoebe did her knitting and her thinking undisturbed; Mary was seldom to be seen, except at meals; the servants wore more dejected faces than ever. These humble mortals, from Mrs. Stroub down, wholeheartedly, if a little covertly, liked her; and now if there was a choice of food in the kitchen it went into Katherine's tray; flowers of the garden's best found their way into Katherine's vases; and at least four half-scared faces looked in each morning, quaintly, hopefully, to smile and wish her well. The twins didn't mind largely because the twins didn't know—though they did appear to wonder a little about the flowers.

One day, from off somewhere, a physician came—a tall brusque extraordinary man dressed for travelling, who left a taxicab waiting two hours at the gate. He asked for Katherine not as Mrs. but as Madam, and he permitted neither the fluttering Milly nor the surprised twins in the sick-room while he was with her. It was a long time, and perhaps, to curious and imaginative ladies, should have been a fruitful one; but though they awaited him primed with questions, he left them as little satisfaction as he had brought.

This was disappointing of course. Since there could no longer reasonably be any doubt of the reality of their guest's illness, they wanted, naturally enough, some information about it—wanted at least to know what it was, whether she would recover, and, if not, how soon she would die. They talked it over at some length in the next few days, with the result, finally, that by their arrangement and before their six attentive eyes, Katherine underwent another examination—this time at the hands of their old friend, Phoebe's doctor. But, for them, this failed too. It was clearly an ordeal for Katherine, and when it was over, the doctor, an observant and sympathetic gentleman for whom in the past she had played and sung and been kind and charming, appeared a little awkwardly and inexplicably to have nothing worth while to tell them. So they talked it over again, and at last resolutely attacked her themselves. She let them down gently, if rather vaguely: her physician, she said, hadn't been very explicit, nor very encouraging. But this, manifestly, was not enough for them, and they kept persistently at her: did she suffer any pain? did she sleep? had she any appetite? how, in general, did she "feel"? and she rewarded their perseverance with reiterations of answers that she had no pain, slept and ate reasonably well, felt only lack of strength—answers that led nowhere and soon grew tiresome. So, finally, so far from giving up, they answered their questions themselves—decided that she must be lying about the pain, that she really felt more than she would admit, that she was dying and knew it—such a doctor would never fail to commit himself of something!—and that she had some mysterious reason for not wanting them to know what she knew about herself—that she was deceiving them, playing for time. Well then, the next step was to discover that reason—to watch her closely, to question her thoroughly on any provocation, to know exactly what information reached her and left her. . . . And so the servants were forbidden to run her errands, the twins opened her letters, and Mary was watched with suspicion and conducted to school by Milly.

The "play" she appeared to be making was no subterfuge. With other eyes they might have seen it as all but pathetically clear of any mystery, must have seen that it was obstinate and courageous and intense only because it was the recognized last play of any kind she was ever to make—the flicker of all that was left in her of the wish and the will to live. Death, to Katherine, could not have been other than deeply, vitally difficult to meet: Katherine was one of those who love most life's loveliness, taste most its sweetness—and lose most in leaving it. And there was Mary. . . .

Doubtless—with her own knowledge of her ailment, and perhaps with some presentiment of its issue—it had been in consideration of Mary far more than of herself that she had come here in the first place—or, at any rate, had stayed. She, certainly, could have chosen better a place to die; but the field could hardly have been broad for the choice of a place for her orphan to live. It must have been bitter indeed at this hour to note how unmistakably this place promised to be abominable for both—bitter particularly on Mary's account. For what, in Heaven's name, would these women do with the child—what, more exactly, would they do *to* her? . . . The question had no doubt been with some insistence present to Katherine for a good while—in all the time at least that she had been hoping, as she must have hoped—counting on it, as she must have counted with all her heart—that they would ultimately soften, would develop, if only on their brother's account, a little the right sort of interest. But they hadn't. Phoebe had almost never seen Mary and of course showed no wish to; Milly eyed her a bit slyly—as a child might some uninvestigated and forbidden toy; and the only real attention yet given her by the twins was this present suspicion of her as an agent in what they chose to consider her mother's deception.

It was then hardly remarkable that Katherine did at last attempt another arrangement for the child's future. She kept Mary home from school one day and managed, with the aid of Mrs. Stroub, to get her out of the house on an errand the twins knew nothing of. About three o'clock that afternoon Milly, idly watching the street, in which for hours nothing had moved but a rain-ridden November wind, leaped up with a squeak and with eyes suddenly wide for what she saw coming up the walk—two Franciscan Sisters. She flew to the twins, and all three flew back to the window. Lucia looked at Emma and Emma at Lucia. Lucia spoke first—"They shan't see her, Sister; they shan't enter this house!"—and together, with Milly after them, they went to the door. . . . A little later, with the visitors gone, the twins downstairs with Phoebe sat waiting, and Milly had gone off to fetch Mary.

The child appeared, large-eyed and looking a little scared. The twins solemnly placed her between them; Phoebe glanced up once from her needles; Milly, hands in lap, craned forward in her chair. Lucia began—"Is your mother expecting company?"

The answer took a moment—"No, Aunt . . ." but it so clearly left something unsaid that they waited for the rest of it—"that is, not exactly company."

"'Not exactly company.' . . Is anybody coming to see her?"

"The Sister Superior might."

"What makes you think she might?"

"Well—Mother said she might."

"Oh. And what does she want to see your mother about?"

Mary took this with some surprise: she looked for all the world as though she might just then, to someone else, have remarked that Aunt Lucia could certainly ask questions, couldn't she? But, "I think," she at last answered, "you ought to ask Mother."

Emma tried now—"Do you know this Sister Superior very well, child?"

"Yes, Aunt—or no, not *very* well. I just sort of know her."

"And do you like her?"

"Oh yes; she's very nice."

"Where does she live?"

"At the Academy, I guess."

"And what sort of place is that—the Academy?"

"Oh—" Mary pondered—"it has a yard with a wall around. And there are all the Sisters, and girls—little ones and big ones, like me; and a big room with little white beds—"

"And should you like to go there—to stay?"

Mary candidly looked at Emma's great eyes, first one and then the other, for some seconds, and then easily dropped, "I think it must be pleasant there."

"A great deal pleasanter than this house, eh?"

"Oh, this is nice too, and you are my aunts and you've been kind to us; but really," quoth Mary, "this is hardly the place for a normal, healthy, impressionable child—" the sentence dwindled quite suddenly to nothing.

"Who says that?"

Perhaps Mary had forgotten hearing anybody say that, but she knew she had gone too far in saying it herself. Emma, without waiting, pressed further—"Well, of course—for a normal, healthy, impressionable child—and so you and your mother decided it would be better for you to go to the Academy to stay than to live here. Isn't that right—eh?"

Mary, her face scarlet, merely looked at her. Emma continued—"And Sister Superior will probably drop in today to see Mother about it—eh? Answer me!"

Mary delayed a little longer—"I'm afraid I don't think I should."

Lucia took it up again—"Have you been out of the house today?"

"Yes, Aunt."

"Where did you go?"

"An errand for Mother."

"What errand?"

"I took a letter."

"*Where?*"

"To the Academy."

"Ah!"

The twins looked at each other; Milly leaned back in her chair; Mary hung her head; and Phoebe, resting her hands in her lap, fixed her eyes upon the child. Lucia broke the silence—"You remember I told you this morning not to leave the house?"

"Yes, Aunt."

"And you disobeyed me!" She turned to Emma—"We must attend to that, Sister. Moreover, she has tried very hard to deceive us here just now. We mustn't overlook these things. She must be taught truthfulness—"

"I didn't lie!"—Mary's confusion had vanished.

Lucia turned upon her a look of withering indignation. Mary met it—"But Aunt, I didn't lie."

The sisters—all four—were astounded; here indeed was pretty behaviour! Lucia opened her mouth to answer—and then didn't. For Phoebe was up, with a suggestion—one hoarse, horrible syllable—"Whip!"

Emma fairly screamed—"Phoebe!—*Sit down!* ... Milly, take the child—quick! ...."

At dinner that evening Mary's chair stood empty. Phoebe was quiet again, the twins seemed satisfied with the day's work, and Milly chattered while nobody listened: the re-established peace of the old days prevailed. But in the midst of the meal the peace was broken: Phoebe's eyes, attracted to the doorway, which she faced, remained fixed and narrowing on an entrant there; the twins, dumbfounded, saw too; and the chattering Milly was suddenly still. Katherine, barefoot and clad only in a night-gown, her face startlingly white against the vivid dishevelled mass of her hair, was approaching the table. She reached Mary's chair, and, leaning there heavily, made them an utterance—weak-voiced, distinct, intense with emphasis—"You punished that child to-day—you hurt her. ... It was wicked—wicked of you ... it proves you capable of the worst I thought of you ... proves you can be cruel to her, that you want to be unjust. ... But—understand me—you are never—*never* to be so again! ... I warn—"

But then one hand went to her mouth to check a cough; she choked; her knees sagged; blood ran from between her fingers; and she crumpled, shuddering, on to the floor.

IV

The difference made in the house by Katherine's death rested, naturally enough, heaviest upon Mary. Whatever it may have represented for the others, to Mary it meant for the present a bewildering, crushing shock, and for the future the loss of most of the companionship, most of the affection, most of the interest, most of the fun, that life had held. As a matter of righteous course, the sisters kept her—fed and clothed her, sent her to school, provided her music lessons, regulated her work and play and meals and sleep, and set Milly to observe and report upon her. If there had been in her any tendency to rebellion, the efficient restraints of this schedule would soon have stifled it. In her room, whence before had issued the only laughter in the house, the old silence prevailed again; where before had been a decent confusion of toys and clothing and books, all was now as neat as even the twins might wish. She took in fact their whole system pretty much as they might wish—turned over to them in pale silence, on demand, her few small jewels; watched with dry-eyed fortitude the replacement of the bright colourful clothes of her mother's choice by the more sombre ones of their own; went without uttered objection to the strange Sunday school where the boys quarrelled and the girls giggled and the poor kind teacher told stories to which nobody listened; accepted unmurmuringly the guardianship of Aunt Milly; even assumed, under their coaching, habits of behaviour far more decorous than natural. . . . Only there were lapses they didn't see—play-times when Josephine, her doll, slipped to the floor forgotten, reading periods when her book lay unopened in her lap, study periods when her page was spattered with tears, hours spent at the piano not in scale practice, but in effort to recall her mother's melodies.

But neither these unhappy little lapses nor the regulations of the twins seemed in any marked degree to check, after the passage of the first black weeks, the revival in her of what most represented the "normal, healthy" child; and in time, though less vivaciously then before, Mary was happy again. "Things happened," said Mrs. Stroub, to make her so. Of these—small things indeed for the most part—Mrs. Stroub's own kind ingenuity was perhaps not seldom itself the source; but they counted up none the less on that account for little Mary. She developed, for one thing, a prideful interest in leaving nothing for her aunts to find fault with, and Mrs. Stroub helped her to enjoy that; also, the good little housekeeper gossiped with her, sewed with her, helped her to augment Josephine's wardrobe, listened with seeming interest to her stories. . . . Then, at Christmas-time there was a tree for her in the quarters of the servants; when spring came, birds nested almost within arm's reach of her window; and in the garden Otis the gardener gave her seeds and a row of her own to plant them in. . . . Also, of course—though it was no such boon as the birds or the flower-bed or Mrs. Stroub—she had the association of Aunt Milly.

*   *   *

That association, after it had lasted a few months, became suddenly and for a good reason even less a boon to Mary than to Aunt Milly herself. At first it would have been difficult to say which of them enjoyed it least: Milly, with her peculiar interests, had little, certainly, to offer for the pleasure or edification of the child—of any child; and Mary was hardly to have been looked to for entertainment of a sort suited to Milly's taste. So they had begun by looking a little more than conscious of having each other rather heavily on their hands; and later, when Mary had grown good-naturedly indifferent about it, and had worked and played and talked and studied and begun her summer's vacation very much as though she were aware only in the faintest way of her aunt's existence, Milly was still making no secret of finding her duty as governess very dull indeed. But the monotony came to an end: one day, on the heels of some accident of talk that revealed a particular phase of Mary's innocence, Aunt Milly changed—appeared all at once to have conceived an interest. The wonder is that, with her eyes, she hadn't seen the pretty little promise of it before!

At any rate, however, she made the most of it now—though always, even while it continued merely a means of amusement, with a kind of caution. She began simply by talking a good deal more with the child, and developed a certain adroitness in turning and keeping the conversation in the vein she liked; she took part in and augmented and varied Mary's amusements to bring into play as much as she could of the child's knowledge and reasoning; above all, amusedly, expectantly, she merely watched—while they walked and talked together, while they played house, while they dressed and undressed Josephine and her companions, while she sat on the edge of Mary's bed and asked her questions—whose answers, to judge by the giggles they provoked, were often enough delightful. She made use even of the child's books, which up to now she had openly despised—volumes all beautiful with colour and gold and pictures—fairy-tales outgrown and already laid aside, books of myths and ballads and medieval tales shaped and toned and glorified to suit the perceptions of a child. Mary knew these well—many almost by heart, and would on the least encouragement dwell endlessly on their passages—enlarging, explaining. . . .

"But Mary," interrupted Aunt Milly on one occasion, "why do you suppose old King Arthur was so put out about Launcelot loving the queen?"

"Oh"—the explanation was ready in an instant—"but he didn't love her the right way. *You know*, Aunt Milly, Launcelot wished she was his wife; and that's not the same as loving her just because she was the queen—is it? It was wrong—*wasn't* it?"

"Oh, I don't know. Maybe he couldn't help it. The king shouldn't have been angry if Launcelot couldn't help it, should he?"

"Oh, but they were guilty—the book says they were!"

"Guilty?—what in the world could they have been guilty of?"

Mary hesitated. She didn't like a question she couldn't answer; and moreover this smacked of an intention of some sort of indignity to three glorious people—"Well—they did *something*."

"Maybe—" Milly wriggled forward in her chair—"maybe the king caught them kissing—or something—". . . But, because doubtless of the now unmistakable indignation in the round eyes before her, Milly let this discussion drop just there.

Mary's reaction to such a passage—and there came to be a good many of them which, like this, ended somehow in the air—was at first an irritating perplexity as to just what Aunt Milly had been driving at. Mary liked to understand things, and in these days Aunt Milly said and did altogether too much that she didn't understand at all. What, for instance, could she have meant one day by all those funny things she said about her birds? what was the meaning of those newspaper clippings she was always bringing to the nursery? why was she always offering books that nobody could possibly enjoy—full of ordinary married people who talked all the time about love! Mary pondered and frowned about it; grew wary of her aunt's efforts to draw her into talk; got angry when, after some embarrassment, she realized that Aunt Milly was making a little fun of her ignorance; and at last concluded that there must be something she didn't know about people—something her mother had neglected to mention, that she didn't for some reason feel free to speak of with Mrs. Stroub, but a mystery to which Aunt Milly, anyway, certainly possessed the key. . . . And so it happened one day that Milly, in the midst of her own angling, found herself silenced by a string of questions as precipitant, as innocently shameless, as atrociously definite, as could well be imagined.

They made for the moment, these questions, a decided difference—enough that Milly wouldn't, in their sweeping completeness, answer them. The frank initiative of the child had the effect—or might have had—of placing their little case squarely in her own small hands; and Milly, who couldn't but foresee the development it might thus attain, clearly didn't want it there. She could after all recognize the unclean face of her culpability, and had sense enough to fear it not a little even while she loved it; and that would be sufficient—for Milly—to determine her to keep her little experiment and all the initiative it was to have precisely under her own thumb. So Mary, now with her aunt's confusion added to the things she had already to wonder about, learned nothing by her questions. Aunt Milly turned her interest, for the present, elsewhere.

Whatever the benefit of this for Mary, it meant for Milly the loss of the best opportunity for enrichment, for the fruition, of her fun, that she was ever to have. Mary's outburst, with its inclusive reach for understanding, had represented hardly less definitely a complete loss of patience—had said but too plainly that she was tired of all these vaguenesses and hints and innuendos, which hadn't always seemed so very nice anyhow! Milly may not have grasped this at the moment, but later—when the time came for her effort to reawaken, on her own terms again, the child's interest—she had to note that the perplexity and embarrassment of before were supplanted by a studied indifference, had to note that Mary too could turn a conversation, that the round little eyes were reading her face, that the clear little mind was learning to anticipate the things she intended to say.

But Milly wouldn't—couldn't, probably, for pride or weakness or disappointment—take this as final; instead, she tried other tactics—treated the child in every possible way as an equal, giggled less frequently, talked more seriously and somewhat more according to Mary's preferences, took to using endearments, to hinting inscrutable promises. And the new method, promising in time some small measure of success, brought them at last to the verge of what might, but for Milly's susceptibility in another direction, have been a definite bit of progress. They had been talking, in the library, for half a summer's afternoon—long enough for Mary to have grown both impatient and a little suspicious; and she had suddenly frankly stated, "But Aunt Milly, I'm sure I don't know what you're talking about again!"

"Oh—" Milly paused—"I suppose I didn't say it very well; but I have a book upstairs that does say it well. I'll get it. You just wait here a minute. It tells about—oh, about everything. We'll read it together—shall we?"

Mary wasn't just sure that they should. She was already tired—more than willing to believe that Aunt Milly's book wouldn't be interesting anyway. Besides, it was glorious outside—and she had, in her garden, "things" coming up! She watched her aunt a little undecidedly out of the room and stood yet another minute thinking and frowning.

Aunt Milly was certainly a funny lady sometimes—especially lately. . . .

When Aunt Milly returned with the book, Mary was in the garden chattering at Otis about bugs.

Milly may have been disappointed, but she had learned well enough by this time that patience, with Mary, made best for insistence. The subject, at all events, would keep, and perhaps tomorrow she should succeed better. So Milly, herself at any rate well enough assured of the fascination of her book, sat down to read alone.

The house was ideally quiet—soundless but for the audible small picking of her finger-nail at the edge of the page as she read. A shaft of sunlight streamed downward through the garden window, shaping upon the floor a slowly changing bright warm parallelogram which accentuated the gloom of the high old shelves and of the room's far corners—in one of which stood Katherine's empty chair that Milly would never occupy. Imperceptibly the patch of light moved. . . . Milly came to the end of a chapter. . . . Far off in the hall a clock struck: it was the hour for Phoebe's nap. The sound of Mary's laugh filtered in now and again with the sunshine— to be followed always by this silence which seemed to grow and to deepen, and which was marred only by the constant picking of Milly's finger-nail at her page. Occasionally she creased one at its upper corner—to facilitate reference, perhaps, for tomorrow; occasionally she allowed herself a little thought upon a passage, or turned back to re-read a page; and occasionally—oddly—her eyes lifted a little waveringly, as though resisting the attraction of someone else's gaze, to look for a moment at Katherine's empty chair. An hour—two hours—passed; the sunlit patch on the floor had narrowed to thinness, had crept to the far wall, climbed it, disappeared; dusk fell in the room. Mary's laugh sounded faintly once more—and Milly rose, book in hand, to go to the window. Perhaps it was only to look out; perhaps she had decided against waiting, after all, until to-morrow; perhaps she intended to call the child in merely to relieve the hateful haunted sense of being alone . . . but with her movement, and although Mary's laugh had passed, the silence ended— gave place to a thrilling faint strange sound of music. . . .

It was the music of an artist's touch—clean; simple, noble—and soft, too, like silence itself, like a sound imagined rather than heard. Milly stood soundless, pale, still; and the music, as from an infinite distance, but still unquestionably from the direction of the music room of this house, marched on—faint, familiar as some deathless dread, full of the character of wind at night, of soundless motion, of stalking shadows: note for note, chord for chord, phrase for phrase—the *Ghost Piece*.

She heard it, this time, through; only when the whisper of the final note had passed did she move. And then it was to fly—to race half frantic from the library through the halls to half a dozen rooms where some-one—anyone—might be, but wasn't. Fairly gasping, she flew upstairs, into the corridor, and brought up there abruptly, face to face with Phoebe.

Milly's fear of her old sister and the fact that they almost never com-municated, by look or word or touch, ceased for the moment to count. She seized Phoebe's arm, gripped it, and stood hysterically crying. Phoebe's eyes, unsurprised—even, noticeably, with a kind of cognizance in them—fixed her own for a long minute, looking deep, before she jerked loose from the pinching fingers, turned about, and drew her quak-ing sister down the corridor and back into her own room. This was a dark place, shuttered, stuffy, forbidding, and on the bed the coverlet had not been smoothed since her nap. There was but one chair; and she shoved Milly into it, and stood before her, staring down and waiting. Milly at length calmed enough—as she must have felt, beneath that gaze, that she was expected to—for a sort of utterance—"She's back—in the house— Ooh, Sister, she's come *back* to this dreadful haunted old place!"

Phoebe didn't answer.

"It's my fault," wailed Milly; "it's my fault!"

Still Phoebe waited—waited until something sufficiently specific had come out about the immediate cause of this distress—until, even, some details had appeared of what Milly had done, as she supposed, to provoke it. And for this Phoebe listened, if anything, more closely than ever— taking everything poor Milly had, aiding her even with an occasional questioning word or two which drew out not only the last invidious de-tails of her sister's experiment, but which, beyond that, seemed precisely to seek substantiation for the apparent significance of what they were both certainly thinking most about—the sudden cogent *opportuneness* with which the intervention had come. Phoebe was clearly forcibly struck by this; she insisted on having it clear; she held poor Milly roughly and rigidly to it, wrung her crooked little mind literally dry of everything that might bear upon it. It took a long time, but it left Milly, certainly, with no more to tell; and when at last it was over, Phoebe abruptly turned her out with the comment that she had been a fool as well as a coward, and with a characteristically persuasive injunction to keep her mouth shut—to tell nobody—not even the twins. . . . Milly, bewildered and still scared, stood whimpering where Phoebe had left her. . . . She had lost her book; but she didn't return to the library to look for it. . . .

As to keeping her mouth shut, she did, for the present, as she had been told; also, from now on, she resumed as much as possible her old habit of staying away from the house. And Mary fell back for companionship, for the moment, upon Mrs. Stroub and Otis and her unspoiled books.

V

Whatever her reason for calling Milly a fool, Phoebe's parting imputation of cowardice was at least natural, from Phoebe: for Milly, fright was of course a serious—a terrible—thing; for Phoebe it probably didn't exist. The dark old lady's mental processes were unknown and largely enough unfathomable; excepting those which Katherine and her music had exposed, no evidence of a susceptibility—save to annoyance—had been known, for years, to escape her; but even so, even with as few signs as had ever appeared by which she might be characterized, no judgment worth the name could ever fairly have imputed to her a susceptibility to fear.

It is hardly to be doubted that, on the day of the music, she had heard it; if she hadn't—if, even, she hadn't unmistakably recognized it— poor Milly would certainly have had to carry her distress elsewhere; and Phoebe had taken it moreover, as their conversation proved, for a signal of the same order as had Milly. But while it was for Milly to go stone cold with horror, it was for Phoebe, recalling, conceivably, a scene with a shawl, to perceive with significant interest that after all Mary's mother, so far from being now, as one would have supposed, beyond reach, was, for the first time since Phoebe had laid eyes upon her, precisely within it— that death, better than any normal condition of life could ever have done, had rendered her accessible and vulnerable . . . that would be the point for Phoebe: her fortuitous, inviting, ready vulnerability. . . .

So it happened that Mary's respite from an aunt's companionship turned out to be short: it all but looked as though Milly had vacated her post simply that Phoebe might fill it. And, certainly, Phoebe filled it abundantly—to the astonishment of Mary, to the increasing uneasiness of everyone else. Not that anything yet showed in her behaviour to provoke alarm; that behaviour consisted, so far, merely in her all but living in company with the child. Her constancy put Milly's to shame: through the windows she watched Mary at play, watched her leave the house, watched for her return; she sat with her through the daily piano practice, knitted with her in the nursery, followed her into the library— and deliberately occupied her mother's chair. Milly heard about it and said nothing and kept away; the twins ogled and whispered and shook their heads and guessed and guessed, and always missed the reason.

The reason, doubtless, was Phoebe's recognized need to know something—as much as she could learn—about Mary. Very likely, in possession of her new-found advantage, she didn't know exactly what to do with it—how to make the most of it; and there was about her whole present business with the child a tentativeness that gave it all the air, simply, of an effort to discover a right lead. Quite possibly the idea of abrupt brutal violence had occurred to her and been put aside—not in the least, of course, because Mary deserved nothing of the kind, but rather because Phoebe would have surmised that violence might not be just the rightly effective thing, for her object, to try. The case did of course prefigure a cruelty of some sort; it was upon the far-reaching efficacy of that very thing—of a cruelty of some sort—that Milly had unwittingly and so convincingly stumbled, and it was precisely there that everything, for Phoebe, had to be built. Only it wasn't by any means certain that one cruelty would be as good as another. The whole potential yield of success lay in a human—in a child's—sensibility; and to waken that, to hurt it most, there must be just one right method. . . . At all events, Phoebe must have thought so; and accordingly, so that she might at the right time know just what means to use—and above all to keep her case, as Milly had in a different way insisted on doing and so astoundingly at last failed, in her own hands—Phoebe could be—indeed had to be—for the present a little patient.

Mary of course, like the twins, didn't know what to make of it—of this difference in Aunt Phoebe; but, unlike the twins, Mary didn't bother very much about it. It had been a little awkward at first—before one had learned to expect for one's efforts to be nice to an old lady the same absence of response as for no effort at all; but the awkwardness soon lost itself in the general odd habit of their intercourse, and thenceforth Mary appeared a good part of the time to have forgotten her taciturn and gloomy old attendant altogether. If, however, there happened to be conversation, Mary made it all; the answers she got were negligible. Phoebe never acknowledged her good-mornings, and seemed simply not to hear the occasional half-shy utterances of admiration for her knitting, or the aimless comment on the weather, or the chatter, which sometimes flowed like a stream, about everything that came into the child's head; but, as was later to be attested by the substance of her first cruel little experiment, the old lady must have been listening all the same.

A good part of Mary's prattle was about her mother—her mother's comradeship, her mother's counsel, her mother's abilities, temperament, clothes, appearance, manners; and Phoebe must have been deaf indeed not to have caught from it the pitch of the child's reverence for her mother's memory. That she had indeed caught it, made sure of it, came out at last conclusively enough. They were on this occasion in the music room—Mary at the piano, Phoebe watching her. The child, delighted with something she had just finished playing, had turned impulsively—"Aunt Phoebe! I did it, I did it—I played it without a *single* mistake!"

Aunt Phoebe may have noticed: her gaze for Mary had an attentiveness that meant something—not approbation, for Phoebe's standard for judging a piano performance was high indeed—but something else, that cooled the child's enthusiasm and made her, after a moment, a little apologetically add—"Of course, Mother played it ever so much better."

The intentness of Phoebe's look deepened by just a shade—as though the accident of that reference to Katherine had made a continuity with her own thinking, had even vivified it for her; and the reflection of the difference, flashed back to Mary almost as an echo of her words, was like a signal, commanding, peremptory, to hold her own thought precisely there—on her mother. So for a full minute they looked thus into each other's face—Mary perfectly still and a little scared, Phoebe with hard, intentional purpose—and with the substance of their thinking as certainly, as distinctly, as intensely Katherine as if she had been there, with them, commanding their attention. . . . Then suddenly, as though for better emphasis for what she had to say, Phoebe leaned forward, her eyes narrowing, her chin out-thrust—"Your mother . . . I *hated* her!"

Poor Mary went white, and after a few speechless seconds under the hot searching old eyes across from her, the tears showed. She kept them back, though, and left the room; it was no place, no occasion, for an answer.

Phoebe watched her out, and sat waiting; but nothing happened. After some minutes she gathered up her knitting and went into the library—to Katherine's chair—and waited. Still nothing happened. She went upstairs to the nursery, which she found empty, and on into Katherine's room; a little later she was back again in the music room, again in the library, and at last, for a restless few minutes, in her own room. There was nothing anywhere for her, evidently; but the expectancy—or whatever it was—with which she moved about, stopped occasionally to listen, sat with her attention visibly in the air, in the near distance, didn't in the least seem to diminish. It was still in her eyes as she watched the averted face of Mary at dinner; later it took her from the company of her sisters—back through all the rooms in which she had waited during the afternoon; it kept her up after the others had gone to bed; and it remained with her when the house was dark and she should have been asleep.

About two o'clock in the morning, so far without sleep, she got up, lit a candle, and sat for a long time on the edge of her bed. The air was cold, and her big shapeless body shivered once or twice in its flannel night-gown. Her feet, marble-white and misshapen with bunions, were slipperless; her hands lay idle at her sides; and her eyes moved back and forth across the room with no attention for what they saw. But if there was uncertainty in her face, and a kind of bewilderment, there was still also its grim determined hopefulness, and not a trace of fear. Downstairs the clock struck half-past two; and she snuffed out her light and went back to bed. Just after three she was up again—in the dark—and now attentively listening. There was a sound in the corridor—someone feeling the way along the wall—the scratch of fingernails across her door had been unmistakable!—and whoever it was was whimpering— like a child. Phoebe opened her door and looked, and saw, near the twins' door, a white figure—a woman, apparently, in night-clothes. She stepped out, and the figure turned at her step and came back towards her. It was Milly, and she was crying. Phoebe, without letting her speak, drew her into the bedroom and closed the door.

Milly continued to weep—much, however, as though she knew she was expected to make no noise—and when she finally spoke it was in a whisper and only half intelligible—"You've done something, you've done something—I don't know what; but you've done something . . . that woman's in the house again. I haven't slept a minute this blessed night! I'll tell the twins—I don't *care*—I will, I will! You can do whatever you like with me . . . Oooh, Sister, if I have to spend another night like this I'll die—I'll die—I'll just die. . . ."

Phoebe watched her, awaiting and at last bluntly demanding an explanation. But the details were vague indeed—". . . I didn't see her— Oh, thank Heaven for that!—and I didn't hear anything. . . . But she's here—she's been here hours. I know it! I've *felt* her—I've *felt* her. And I know it's something you've done. The child was crying in her room when I came up to bed—when she should have been asleep. . . . Oh, I'm going to *tell*—I'll tell the twins, the servants—everybody—"

But she didn't. Phoebe kept her the rest of the night, and when daylight came Milly had changed her mind. From the time they went downstairs, however, until Milly had left the house for the day—a wet dismal fall day—Phoebe never let her out of sight; and then, with her knitting, she went to the nursery.

Mary was not there—very likely because she suspected that Aunt Phoebe would be. But she might better have saved herself the trouble of hiding. Phoebe could wait, without doubt, longer than Mary would be able to avoid her; and Phoebe, moreover, would hardly be gentler for having been made to wait. The night just past had revealed—or had seemed to reveal—the first faint signs of what the old lady had meant, in her vindictive purpose, to evoke; and Phoebe, of all women in the world, would want them verified. What it would take to verify them, what form any manifestation could take that would define, with anything like the certainty she would require, the unearthly antagonism she wanted, Heaven alone knew; but Phoebe would face that: it was her challenge—a challenge from which something, certainly, was to be expected! She waited now, at all events, with growing impatience, staring out into the rain which must surely be keeping the child somewhere indoors, prowling through her room, frowning at the gorgeously attired Josephine, wandering occasionally through other rooms where Mary might be. . . . At lunch, Mary managed not to look at her, and afterwards disappeared again. Phoebe went to the music room: the child had her practicing to do and would surely come there. But she didn't; and when the hour for her nap came, Phoebe, without having yet caught sight of the truant, trudged off as usual to her room, leaving an unfinished collar on which she had been at work lying in her chair.

Not long afterward, then, Mary appeared, looking up and down the corridor and tiptoeing her way from Mrs. Stroub's door to her own. In the nursery she sat down, listless, dejected: for a "normal, healthy" child, this was all very bewildering and trying, to say the least. . . . She stood up, looked aimlessly about, went to the window, down which outside the rain still streamed; then she replaced one by one the things Phoebe had pulled out and left lying; and at last she sat on the floor to talk over with Josephine this incomprehensible business about Aunt Phoebe. Next to her mother and Mrs. Stroub, Josephine stood incontestably first of all the world in Mary's affections. She might, but for the small matter of her deafness, have heard a good many more or less interesting details this afternoon of what Mary thought about Aunt Phoebe's behaviour, and about other things; for Mary, once started, and conveniently indifferent to Josephine's limitations, said a good deal. And in the midst of it the door opened and Phoebe entered. It was now upwards of thirty hours since she had slept.

The marks of her weariness showed plainly as she stood above the wide-eyed child and her doll; it seemed to weight down her face, to have made it heavier, left it yellower, deepened its lines and its grimness. Mary only looked at this face—but looked afraid. There is no knowing what Phoebe intended at that moment, what she might have done if Mary hadn't, as though to protect Josephine, slid the doll off her lap and around on to the floor behind her—out of Aunt Phoebe's reach. But Phoebe noticed the motion, and within a second had stooped and caught up the doll, looked at it once, lifted it high, and dashed it violently to the floor. The head broke into a hundred bits, the weighted eyes flew across the room, the flaxen wig rolled back limp and upside down, and the trunk in its silken dress lay on its back with arms outspread at Mary's feet. . . .

The child had sprung up, but now, while Phoebe looked and listened as for something else, she knelt and lifted her doll, gathered the
scattered fragments of its head into the apron of her dress, picked up
the wig, recovered even the eyes, and laid them all upon her bed. She
had forgotten Aunt Phoebe, and as she gazed at what was left of Josephine her tears fell unchecked, unashamed, unnoticed. Phoebe, with
the passage of several uneventful minutes, disappointedly sank into a
chair. Mary still paid no attention, until her aunt, looking too tired to
move, spoke—"Get my knitting—in the music room."

Mary, with astonishment in her stricken little face, turned to stare;
Aunt Phoebe didn't as a rule ask things of people, and now, of all
times. . . . But Mary went for the knitting—for nobody ever opposed
Aunt Phoebe, either. She returned in a few minutes and laid the knitting in Phoebe's lap—but not the collar, not the exquisite little thing
she had herself admiringly watched the growth of in the old lady's
hands. This piece appeared to be a shawl—handsome enough too, but
scorched and burnt in places, as though it had been in a fire. Phoebe's
eyes bulged as she looked at it; but she shook it out, held it up—to
make sure. . . . "*Where was this?*"

Mary, watching her, had backed away towards the door, which was
slowly swinging, open—"In your chair, Aunt . . . in the music room."

Phoebe looked again at the shawl, at Mary, back at the shawl, and
her face changed. The astonishment faded, and her eyes flamed and her
mouth twisted and her veins swelled with fury. . . . Then suddenly she
was up, making for Mary; but Mary was gone, and Aunt Phoebe
brought up against the firm oak door, which had in that instant
slammed between them.

The child ran, sobbing, half choking, straight to Mrs. Stroub; and
Mrs. Stroub, knowing, doubtless, the limits of the protection she could
offer, took her to the twins. And they listened, and questioned, and
pondered, and didn't, for once, know what to do; it was no easy matter
to deal with Sister Phoebe. But after draining the child, thrice over, of
all she had to tell, and telling each other for the tenth time that they
must question Sister Phoebe that evening, they excused Mary from appearing at dinner and told her to be on hand in the parlour at half-past
nine in the morning, "sharp." The twins were methodical ladies.

But they got nothing out of Phoebe that evening. She glowered at
them across the table, said not a word, and spent the evening prowling
about the unoccupied rooms of the house. At eleven o'clock, to the obvious relief of everybody, she went to bed.

If she had so far been unsatisfied, had wanted some clearer signal,
some definite evidence, that the thrusts she had made at Mary had

gone, as she had intended, beyond the child, the uncertainty could pass and the want be stilled at last. She was but just in bed when the air of her room was filled with all she need require of evidence—filled as the library had been on that other day for Milly, with the sound of music. It had no emphasis particularly, no loudness, no apparent intention; it was simply unmistakably there. The old lady hadn't yet lain down, and now apparently she couldn't, but sat listening, awed in spite of the gross expectancy of these last two days into statue stillness. The music went on for several minutes and then quietly stopped; but even in the silence she sat there rigidly upright, still listening. At last, though, with a sudden show of decision, she got down from the bed and stole downstairs—to peer as in other days through the curtains of the music room—to go in—and to find nothing except the silent lifeless furniture. . . . She came heavily back and got once more into bed. But she was not permitted to sleep: hardly had her head settled upon the pillow when the sound came again. Unsurprised this time, she didn't wait—had even reached the foot of the stairs before the music stopped; but this time as before the music room was empty. She looked elsewhere now, however, into several other rooms, before returning upstairs; but met everywhere only darkness and stillness and the deepening damp chill of the house. She must have decided, after this, not to come downstairs—not to listen even, perhaps—if the music should sound again; for when, as she lay down for the second time, it did sound again, she determinedly didn't move. As though to compel her, then, its character changed: before, it had consisted of aimless little passages which might have done nothing more than barely hold her attention—keep her awake; now it swelled into authentic, robust, commanding music— marching majesties of Bach, the fine old beauty of Gluck, and soaring glory of Beethoven—and Phoebe, fascinated and helpless, sat upright again, drew up her knees, and listened—listened with all her soul and all her mind—frowned and irresolutely moved with the old growing greedy uneasiness which meant that what she got thus was not enough—was not *enough*. She climbed down at last from her bed, and going cautiously, as not to lose a note, crept downstairs, through the intervening rooms—and abruptly, just as she reached for the curtains, the music stopped. . . .

So for hours it continued. One o'clock came, two, three—and Phoebe got no rest. Dishevelled and haggard, she looked ready to collapse; her hands shook; her feet all but dragged as she moved about— sometimes in the dark, sometimes in the full light of the lamps, sometimes grotesquely shadowed by a candle. Early in the night, after those first astonished minutes, she had seemed for a space to enjoy her first real satisfaction in months. But that had passed long since, and as the night had lengthened and her weariness deepened and deepened, her face had lost its expressionless hardness, its customary dark inscrutability, and hung flabby and twitching, concealing nothing, betraying helplessly the effects of the night's march of torment. . . . First it had been the growth merely of an annoyance, of a wish that the game might stop; this had deepened into an apprehensive nervousness; then there had been signs of a decision, a resolve to hold up, to see through unshrinkingly whatever it was that she had to see; later she had wavered again, shown bewilderment, worry, desperation; and finally had come a sharp—a forced—revival of that resolve. She seemed to grasp at the supporting firmness of this, to hold to it as the minutes passed with all the strength of her incorrigible old soul—as though it were the only thing that would keep her wits together. She crouched motionless on the edge of her bed labouring to keep it up, with sweat dripping from her face, with her eyes—burning, bloodshot, wide in one second, half-closed the next—fixed immovably upon nothing, with her ears full of the quickening, swelling, sweeping, relentless rhythm of the music. . . .

But she had nerves, and four o'clock brought the limit of what they would stand: control, resolution were suddenly gone, and in their place rose another mad surge of fury. She stood up, towering still for an instant, and then was in the corridor, hurrying—lurching and swaying as she went—towards the nursery. Her hands were empty—but Phoebe's hands were strong! They found the knob of Mary's door, turned it, and the next second they were groping at Mary's pillow. The music downstairs had stopped.

The bed was empty. Phoebe straightened up for a second's uncertainty and then crossed to the door opening into the room where Mary's mother had died. This door stuck a little, but she wrenched it open, stepped on to the threshold, looked in—stopped. . . . A gasp died in her throat. . . .

VI

When Mary's promised questioning began next morning, Phoebe was absent. Milly was on hand, however, looking pale and saying nothing. She had, since coming down, appeared a little to be waiting for someone else to say something—something particular; and she had looked sharply, with quickened expectancy, at Mary when during breakfast the child had remarked that she and Mrs. Stroub had been unable to sleep—that several times they had thought they heard the piano.

Mary's heavy eyes confirmed what she said; but neither of the twins appeared to notice.

The inquisition turned out to be by far the severest Mary had yet stood: the twins had, by all the signs, reached some conclusions before it began. They required her first to recount in detail everything that had passed in the last weeks between her and Phoebe. They told each other openly that their sister's remark of two days ago, about the child's mother, and the breaking of the doll yesterday, were enough to have provoked in her a feeling of resentment, even of vengefulness; and it was evident they expected Mary to appreciate the generosity of this admission. Finally they undertook to extract from her a confession that would come easier because she knew they held the motive for her supposed offence in a measure pardonable—a confession that she had replaced Phoebe's collar with that shawl. They were sure—of course—that Katherine had, long ago, given it to her; so sure that Mary's denial, her protestation that until yesterday she had never so much as seen the shawl, but too plainly deepened their conviction of her guilt. No doubt they were pleased with the simple sagacity that had aided them to their conclusion—which, certainly, no contradiction of a mere slip of a child should be permitted to shake. So for an hour they got nowhere; and it turned out, as their pleasure in its difficulty grew, to be a cruel business indeed for little Mary. They set traps that she all but stumbled into, they tired her, bewildered her, provoked her to impatient answers, rebuked her for impudence, took her vexed tears for harbingers of a confession, began all over again, and looked aghast and severe indeed when at last, stamping her small feet, she covered her face with her hands and burst distractedly into tears. The good ladies exchanged a glance here: this, surely, was the beginning of the end. . . . But they had reckoned without Milly.

Milly's prejudice in the case might readily enough have sprung from the fact that she was, in one sense at least, normally humane; but more persuasive than its mere injustice must certainly have been, for her, its other, deeper, latency. At any rate there had been more than once during the morning a sympathetic softening in her queer little face as she watched the child; she had cast severe glances—severe indeed for Milly!—at her sisters; she had, from the beginning, worn the look of an expectancy distinctly different from theirs; she had grown nervous with the increase of the child's bewilderment; and the tension which in Mary had broken with hysterical tears had had, it appeared suddenly at last, a parallel as little supportable in Milly as in the child herself. But with Milly the reaction was not a collapse. She was suddenly on her feet, her face aflame, all but yelling at her sisters—"Emma! Lucia!—stop it—

stop it *now*—this minute! You don't know what you're doing! . . . Mary, stop crying—go away—go and practice. They're not going to ask you any more questions now. Emma, send her out—tell her you're through with her!"

The twins, doubtless too astounded to do anything else, sent the child off—to await their call in the music room; and Milly, hardly able to contain herself until Mary was out of earshot, then burst out—"The child didn't play that trick—*didn't*—I *know* it. Her mother did!—No, don't stop me; I say her mother did it! Oh, it isn't all she—it isn't the first thing she's done. She's been in this house for weeks—maybe for months. I *know* it: I ought to know it, Heaven knows. . . . She's done things!—she stopped me from—from . . . I tried—I—I told the child things—I set her to thinking about—about—I tried to make her like myself—as nasty as myself; and her mother—her *mother*—prevented me. I heard her, as distinctly as I hear myself this minute, playing on the piano—Oh yes, it was she—it was, it was! Nobody else could—. . . I told Phoebe—I was afraid, almost frantic—Phoebe was the first person I met. She made me keep still—she threatened me—made me promise. That was weeks ago. Phoebe's been watching the child ever since—you know—you've seen—trying to decide on the best—the worst—way to hurt her. Phoebe hated her mother—hates her yet—and Phoebe's not afraid. She'd kill the child—Oh, you know she's capable!—to hurt her mother. Day before yesterday she made that mean remark—offended that baby, frightened her, made her cry. Well, she's been driven nearly crazy since. She hasn't slept a wink—just ask her!—she can't rest. Mary's mother was in the house night before last—all night—as surely as you sit there. I know she was—I felt her—I couldn't sleep—I nearly went mad. At three o'clock in the morning I was coming to you—to tell you—but Phoebe caught me and made me stay with her. Yesterday . . . that doll; and you know what happened with the knitting. But the child didn't—*didn't*—do that! Last night that woman was here, playing on the piano, again; I heard her—five times. But it's not for me, now; it's for Phoebe—for Phoebe. I haven't hurt the child; I'll never think of hurting her again—and, mark my words, no harm shall ever come to her from any of us! Her mother warned us—remember?—the day she died?—the first time you punished the child?—warned us not to be cruel to her, not to be unjust? Well, we've been cruel; we've been unjust—all of us: it was cruel of me—what I did; it was unjust of you to take away her pretty things, make her almost a servant; and Phoebe's worst of all. . . . We hated her mother—you know it as well as I—we were glad she died, glad to be rid of her; but we're *not*—we're not rid of her! She's here! We've been fools enough to bring her back; and she'll stay; she'll haunt us, drive us crazy, unless we do what's right. Just wait!—just wait! She'll make you give back those pretty dresses; she'll make Phoebe—"

However that might have been, something about her old sister struck Milly forcibly enough to silence her as, at this moment, her eyes met those of Phoebe herself. The old lady's appearance was enough, indeed, to have arrested a good deal less susceptible person than poor Milly, who, with the twins, stood now astoundedly staring at her. Phoebe hadn't dressed—wore only slippers and a woollen bath robe; her legs obeyed her badly; she trembled, as with a chill; her face, partly veiled by a tangled hanging mass of hair, was livid, aged, hideous. . . . Milly, after the first minute, wouldn't look at her; but the twins got her a chair, and she sat in it. She hardly noticed any of them; her eyes, which were hard and steady enough, swept the room, looking for something else. Lucia, a little uncertainly, tried to catch her attention— "Sister Phoebe, you're not well; you should—"

Phoebe interrupted—"Where's that child?"

Lucia ignored the question, changed her subject—"We questioned Mary this morning, about yesterday—about the shawl. She denies having given it to you, in place of your collar, as a—a trick. . . . It seems we don't understand quite everything. Milly has just told us—just said that the child isn't really responsible—that—that her mother is. It's incredible of course; but Milly thinks—appears quite certain—that the mother, in some manner, has *been* here—" Lucia groped; Phoebe watched her. "Milly assures us," Lucia went on, "that you will confirm what she says—that, even last night, you probably had evidence— probably heard the woman—"

Phoebe helped her out—"Heard her!—I *saw* her."

The effect of this, for sheer amazement, was almost as though the experience had been their own: it left them, for seconds, speechlessly staring into one another's faces; and Phoebe, forgetting them, got to her feet and started for the far door—two rooms beyond which lay the music room. Emma, recovering first—though even so a little late— attempted to stop her; but Phoebe, as little as ever to be intercepted, pushed her aside—violently, so that she staggered. The others were up now too—Milly trembling, Lucia pale with apprehension but still able to scream—"Milly, run for Otis, quick—*quick!*"—and as Milly bolted, Lucia tried to pass Phoebe—to reach Mary first. The effort failed: Phoebe faced about with raised hands, and, with her eyes playing warningly between their blanched faces, walked backward to the threshold of the music room—and, still facing them, passed on in. Lucia seized the curtains, to follow; but, inside, Phoebe held them closed.

Wide-eyed now with dread, the twins looked at each other—and as their eyes remained fixed and that firm irregularity in the curtains still held them excluded from within, seconds passed, heavy and deathly still, and they stood helpless. . . . They might have wondered why Phoebe waited, why *she* stood thus still, holding the curtains at her back, and facing within—merely looking across the room, at the piano—or, perhaps, at Mary. . . .

But if they wondered, it was at most for but a minute, for now, beginning with both at once and growing by quick degrees, there came into their faces a change. The dread, the fearful expectancy, faded; and in its place came a look of uncertainty, of doubt, of wonder, of mounting excitement—as though, strangely, their attention had shifted, had left Phoebe, left the threatened child, for another interest—for an interest whose issue, yet to be determined, was of the greatest, of the deepest, significance. . . .

Whether they recognized the difference or not, they could hardly have escaped it. Not only they, but the very air was charged, was verily chilled, with it. They faced each other now in an atmosphere not of horror but of conflict, silent, intense, vital; and it held them trembling and tensely waiting. . . .

The curtains moved—fell into straight natural folds; Phoebe had let them go. There was a step—two, three, four, five steps—slow and heavy; then silence again—silence deepening and thickening every instant with this intense incomprehensible charge of struggle, of impending disaster. Phoebe must now be near the centre of the room—must be standing quite still. No sound came from Mary—no word, no cry. . . . but suddenly, shockingly, in Phoebe's voice—*"Don't touch me!"*

No clear, calm, imperious words these, like Katherine's on that other occasion; they rushed out harsh, coarse, merely loud . . . and after them, after another instant's stillness, there came a gasp, the sound of a heavy fall. . . .

For another second the twins' eyes held; then, in the clearing air, they seemed to relax, to awake; and Emma, throwing aside the curtain, entered the music room. Phoebe lay face down upon the floor; and across the room, her face streaked with the paths of tears, lay Mary, sound asleep in a great chair. The twins, kneeling over their sister's body, let the child sleep. . . . she hadn't, evidently, any need of *them*.

Part 2
The Lady who listened

The doctor probably felt, scanning the undecided faces of his hostesses, that they would after all grant what he had asked; for, as he had had time hopefully to reassure himself while waiting for his hat, they had indeed remarkably changed. His plea, made this afternoon with the support of his quarter-century of friendship with them, made none the less eloquently because he had frankly admitted it to be a bit unusual, had at all events carried all the sincerity, all the persuasion, he had been able to put into it. He had done, certainly, all he could—except now, standing in their veranda, surveying contemplatively the wide visible expanse of their grounds, to turn to them with a final hopeful word—"I hope you'll take him in. Your house—this wonderful outdoor peacefulness—is really just the thing, just everything, he needs. Please consider it. I urge you to."

He left them then—to meet however, almost at once, with another opportunity to speak for his patient. Milly had heard him at some length an hour before in the parlor; but she overtook him now at the gate to hear him, if possible, again—to make sure no single available detail had escaped her in the house. As happened, however, she had a little to wait; the doctor, with a question of his own, spoke first—"Do you think they'll let him come?"

Milly accepted the check with reluctance—"I hardly know. But I wanted to ask—"

"They've changed so!" pursued the doctor;—"changed, I think, remarkably. Why, ten years ago—!" But he left this, as an expression of what must *then* have happened to his request, unfinished. . . .

"Ten years ago," Milly briefly volunteered, "they—well, couldn't have changed."

His rejoinder, coming slowly, both made and invited amplification—"Because, you mean, of Phoebe."

She nodded; and then a little hurriedly, as though now finally to dispose of the topic, completed her theory—"And since then I guess they couldn't very well have helped it—because of Mary."

But the doctor was not to be hurried, the topic not yet to be set aside—"It's been, as a substitution of influence, extreme, hasn't it? But I suppose that even if she were less charming than she is, her living here—growing up in the house, and all that—would inevitably have made *some* differences."

If there seemed for an instant a peculiarly direct implication in this last emphasis, Milly's quick glance at him discovered no suggestion that it had been meant for her; and in another minute she had reluctantly but in spite of herself read into it, rightly or not, another significance—"'*Some* differences'—but not quite all you seem to see, eh?"

With no sign either of denial or admission, he turned to face her; and she, visibly with more patience than comfort in their subject, continued slowly her explanation—"Well, it's true that at first—before we had learned to love the child enough to be kind to her on that account—they—we—did recognize a sufficient reason at least for being careful of her!"

As he still didn't reply, she looked for a moment away from him, and then, with face still averted, abruptly, nervously, finished—"I mean because we were afraid—*afraid*—not to be careful. You may smile at that, and the twins might too, now; but *I* can't smile at it, even yet . . . !" She faced him again—"Please, can't we change the subject now?"

By way, perhaps, of atonement he allowed her then to make it what she would; and she made it, of course, the temporarily blinded boy whom the doctor hoped to place for a final convalescence in the sisters' house. He showed her, during the next half hour, a good deal more consideration than she had just shown him; but her questions, reaching for every thinkable detail of the young man's case, history, habits, personality, ended, as the doctor had doubtless expected, by exhausting at last his patience. He rose decisively then from their bench—"You see, Miss Milly—as I told your sisters—my part of the boy's case has only to do with his eyes. The man who's had him—for his nerves, I mean—let me bring him here almost altogether because I could promise just the right environment. Even while we talked it over I had this house of yours in mind—down to the very room—"

"Room? Which room?"

"The one Miss Phoebe used to have would do—would be exactly suitable. It's dark there, as I remember, and the light could be regulated very well to accustom his eyes to it. . . . But, as I told your sisters, he's really practically well—only he does need, for a time, quiet and regularity, such as he would find here. He's been in somebody's hands, under somebody's care, for a long time, and his independence must begin a little easily. That's all . . . and really"—he laid his hand on the gate—"he ought to come here."

Milly still wondered—"Then there's nothing odious about him; I mean he's not eccentric—or stupid—or—?"

"Far from it! If anything, his mind's a bit too much awake—too active. Why"—he smiled directly at her—"before you've had him a week he'll know you—all of you—through and through, even though he can't see you. . . . You'll find he's anything but stupid."

"Is he good looking?"

The doctor laughed outright—"Handsome!" . . . But as she watched him down the street Milly's look bespoke a curiosity still not wholly satisfied.

There was to be a sufficient interval, before the decision of the twins was reached, for her curiosity and her interest to sharpen; and by that time, for Milly, the prospect of the young man's coming—the promise, in particular, of interests bound to arise from a masculine presence—had gained considerably in attractiveness. The twins of course had their own different view, and saw small reason, for compliance, in Milly's; but Milly, seeing as little, for objection, in theirs, supported the doctor, urged their consent.

They gave it at last; and so, blindfolded and in the care of their pleased old friend and a humble little valet whose name was Matthew and who looked respectfully askance at all these women, the young man came. Milly was afidget with eagerness; Mary, interested and faintly amused; the twins, sharply observant and quaintly stiff and proper. While they talked Milly, from a corner, took a not wholly satisfying measure of the boy, whom the doctor even now called simply Richard. His full name, a first detail for Milly, she liked; but his appearance fell somewhat short of what the doctor's "handsome" had seemed to promise. Milly's predilection was for plump pink men with curly hair; and this one was thin and tall, had straight hair, and his chin and nose and forehead looked bloodless and far too angular. She wondered about his eyes, and decided they must be dark, like his hair—wondered whether he would always be as shy as he appeared to be now—liked the perfection of his clothes—noted that his hands were long and white, as she understood a gentleman's should be—and she was struck, as indeed they all seemed to be, by the richness of his voice. Not that he used it much on this occasion: it appeared to embarrass him to talk, as he had to do, into the middle of the room and at nobody in particular. . . .

But the important point was that the twins, who had scanned him fully as closely as had Milly, seemed to approve him; so his stay was assured. They hadn't in the least, however, with their precise speeches, let him know they approved him. It was only after the interview was over, after he had thanked them briefly and a little as though he didn't quite know how much gratitude he ought to express, that he was given a distinct sign of welcome. Mary accompanied him, with the doctor and Matthew, to the room he was to occupy—Phoebe's old room, as the doctor had wished. There, at the door, while the others were busy inside with his things, she said, "It's hardly fair not to tell you we're glad you've been able to come. . . . I hope you'll like us."

"I'm sure I shall; it's extremely kind of you to take me in. . . . But you must forgive me—" he seemed eager to get this said—"if I appear confused as to which of you is which. I have to depend entirely upon my ears, you know. I didn't hear your voice downstairs, did I?"

"No. I'm Mary."

"Mary. . . . But of course I can't—"

"Oh but you must. You see, we all have the same name, except our first names. We're all—uh—elderly maiden ladies."

"Elderly—?"

"Not one of us would tell her age for the world!"

He smiled—and so, from the depths of Phoebe's room and with beaming gratitude, did the doctor.

I

The doctor's assurance to the sisters that his patient would give them no trouble was so well verified that in a very short while their concern for him was reduced to the single small question of what he did, in his detachment, with his time. The twins, who had been dubious on a dozen points about taking him in, were evidently content: the changeless march of their life had sufficed for them for so long that they were doubtless better satisfied than not to have it go on unaltered. But Milly was disappointed. She had expected some change, something new, different, interesting; had done, even before the boy came, a quantity of thinking about him; had been solicitous, since, of his comfort; had schemed to enlarge his contact with herself, with the twins, with Mary; had tried to be friendly with him—had tried as far as she might even to be friendly with Matthew; had watched the two men, wondered about them, followed them, listened to them . . . but her interest and her efforts had come to nothing. They provided opportunity in plenty for mere observation—spent long periods sitting or walking in the grounds; but one seldom heard their voices unless one compelled them to speak; and it wasn't, after a time, so very interesting to get nothing out of them but politeness, or to watch them from a distance, walking, walking, walking, all the time! . . . And so, disappointingly in Milly's view that had been so eager, it dwindled to a rather flat situation after all—in which her interest became at last more than anything else a kind of vague hope that something would happen to alter it.

She was later to discover, with a shock, that something had happened—was to feel herself suddenly a little sick with the realization that, under her very nose, something of the most engaging sort had been, and was still, going on that she knew nothing about. This conviction, at once vexatious and sharply pleasant, was the quick result for her of a small scene witnessed one afternoon from her bedroom window. She had been watching Richard feeling his way about with a stick in the grounds below—been following idly and for the hundredth time his blind pacings and practicings and difficulties which had so largely lost their interest—when her attention was caught by Mary entering the grounds from the street. The girl, spying the boy from near the gate, approached him directly across the lawn. Milly straightened, leaned closer to the window to watch them—saw him stop to listen while Mary was yet at some distance, saw swift smiles of greeting, watched them talk—easily, familiarly, as friends—saw her, apparently on his suggestion, turn him about, saunter at his side to a bench, and sit down with him. Here, as Milly greedily looked, the girl unwrapped a package she had carried, and placed in his hands a small book. He held it a little helplessly as she none too purposefully rose from the bench; and then, in response evidently to his having asked her, she resumed her place beside him, took the book, and began to read. She was still with him when, half an hour later, the appearance of Matthew ended the reading; and they entered the house together.

*   *   *

If this little passage meant but a tenth of what Milly's interpretation saw in it—if, as she was at once certain, it could be taken as proving that a "romance" was afoot—a romance which had unaccountably and most provokingly got off to a start well ahead of her—the romance might be said to have gained yet another pace on the day, not long afterward, of the scene's sequel. On this occasion, which Milly was not at home to witness, Mary had again met Richard in the grounds, and he had after two minutes reached into his pocket to draw out her book—"I've kept my promise to have Matthew read to me from this; but Matthew's reading . . ." he paused a moment, and then—"If you have time—or if you don't mind—"

Mary took the book—"But I may be as bad as Matthew."

"I'll be judge."

She gave him, during the next half hour, ample opportunity for that; and when she had at last closed the book and they had talked a little about it, she stayed easily on while their subject changed and their talk drifted and paused and progressed and occasionally quite lapsed altogether. Neither seemed to mind the silences: they fell in, perhaps, too beautifully with the quiet of the day—with a certain charmed clearness and stillness that lay like a spell upon the grounds. . . . But if the serenity helped their silences, it at last also helped their talk—perhaps even in a measure provoked, in Richard, the beginning of what was to be their last free exchange of the day—"I was just thinking that I ought to say something—make some substantial expression of gratitude—to your aunts. Their house—or at least these grounds—have been a godsend . . . especially"—his voice changed a little with his emphasis— "especially these grounds. They've kept my interest—have actually done me good—from the first time I walked in them. I've explored them from end to end; I know all the trees, how many paces it takes to cover every walk; when the sun is hot I can almost read the very sundial; and I've wondered very often about that fountain at the west side—whether it ever plays." He paused, but he wasn't, clearly, waiting for her answer, and Mary said nothing. "And then," he resumed, "there's something else. My eyes, when I see again, will probably show me wonders in the colours and details and mass of it all—will make huge differences in my imagined picture of it; but there's something that won't be changed. . . . I mean I feel sure that whatever I see, whatever differences my seeing makes, won't—can't—change my impression of what I recognize as the place's character: I can't believe that it could possibly look its peculiarly consistent peacefulness and friendliness more abundantly than it has made me feel them. It's unusual, and I don't describe it at all well; but I've encountered it too often now to doubt it— even if I wished; and I don't wish that at all! It's here always—like— like the presence of a good spirit—to make one welcome . . . but does that sound too fanciful?"

Mary's answer showed how little she thought so—"No . . . but it's— it seems remarkable that your impression should be, in this short time, so distinct. There's no doubt of—well, of what you call its character— the friendliness, the good spirit; I've felt that too, but have always just accepted it, I suppose, as—as a feature of this being my home. Doesn't one's home mean more, in just that way, than other places?"

Quietly, unhurriedly, he thought it over. "But that wouldn't explain it for me, would it?—wouldn't say why the sunshine strikes deeper for me here, and the feel of the ground and the sounds of the trees mean something more than they've ever meant for me anywhere before. . . ." He paused a little, and continued, "But tell me something. Is your feeling toward the house—or rather is the feeling you have *of* the house— quite the same? Is there, inside, in the same degree as here, the peace, the assurance of welcome, the—"

Mary interrupted: Aunt Milly had just entered the gate, had seen them—"Not entirely; not in all the rooms. In my own it's better, stronger, clearer than anywhere—more distinct even than here. But my explanation holds there above all: that room is mostly, mostly home— mostly mine; it was my mother's before it was mine and my father's even before that. . . . How," she went on interestedly, a little hurriedly, "do you find the house, inside?"

"As much as I'm familiar with" (Milly's step was already audible) "distinctly different!"

II

Milly's feelings, as she hurried across the lawn toward them that day, had been nothing if not mixed. Curiosity had seized her the moment she saw them; she had turned to join them against a flicker of decent reluctance, which at once gave place to a bitter little vexation with herself for having gone out; and then had come the rush of a stream of supposition as to what they had been saying and doing while she was gone.

What that supposition amounted to, and what all her observation and thinking for days to come seemed to support, was a strengthening of her suspicion of the day of the book—that irritating conviction that something "romantic" had happened and she had missed it. Milly's disappointment was as natural as it was genuine. She had only to see, only to think she saw, the signs of that particular trend in any contact of male with female to be seized with a kind of ecstasy of eagerness to see, to hear, to know, all there was to be seen or heard or known about it. And here, as she wishfully made it out, was just such a case—placed for all its progress under her very nose, to be enacted by people she knew—whose motives she could expect to understand—whose feelings, even, she might hope to share; yet here while still in its beginnings it was escaping her . . . !

She nevertheless made, however, with what success she could, the best of it; and if the things she took care henceforth not to miss—the contrived constancy of her young friends' companionship, the softness of their speeches and the play of their smiles as they talked together, the whole growing evidence of their falling helplessly in love with each other—if these pretty little signs didn't please her into forgetting her first disappointment, they at least decidedly sharpened her curiosity, prompted her to abandon every interest but this, and kept her constantly, hungrily, on the watch. . . . And so it happened that she was able one afternoon to carry her niece a bit of information: "Mary, I'm afraid your gentleman's love for our grounds is going to get him into trouble if he isn't careful. He's been outside in this miserable weather for an hour, walking, walking—"

Mary went to a window—to see, dimly visible through the mist and with his rain clothes shining with wet, the striding tall figure of Richard. Two minutes later, from under her umbrella, she watched his face— drawn, colourless, sharp-lined as it hadn't been since his first days with them—while he explained—"It's—it was—I felt depressed—I really felt I couldn't stay there, in my room, any longer. . . . I've been nervous. . . ."

"But you could have come downstairs—you know that." Then, as she hurried him houseward—"Were you alone up there? Where was Matthew?"

"Oh, Matthew—!"—they had reached the house—"something's gone wrong with Matthew. He's taken to deserting me. . . . And now"—when she had disposed of his cape—"what are you going to do with me?"

What she did with him was to act on Milly's suggestion that he be taken into the library where there was a fire and he could dry his feet. Milly followed them from the door, and immediately, in the girl's quick understanding of his first words in the library, found something to wonder about—the perplexity this time turning upon the question of what must have passed between them in some previous conversation with which this first exchange of theirs made so smooth a continuity. On the threshold of the great dim high-shelved room he had stopped, lifted his blinded face as to look up—smiled—"How wonderfully distinct it is here! . . ."

"Yes. This is quite the best, the friendliest, of them all—except my own. And the reason—for me—" Mary went on—"is still the same."

"Because it's simply home, you mean—?"

"Because it's a little more than simply home. My mother was very fond of it. . . . You're remarkably impressionable," she quietly concluded.

"Too much so," he agreed, "—at times. But," he smiled again, "your house—some of it—is remarkably impressive."

They talked of something else then, and Milly was left uncomfortably in the dark about what they had meant. She stayed with them, however, and listened with all her ears to what they said, and wondered what they were thinking about in their silences, until at last, as an indirect result of some allusion to music, it came out that Richard had been hesitating for a considerable time to ask the use of the piano. Resolved, then, to stay in the library until their return—even though she must hear every dreaded note—Milly watched them go off together to the music room. . . . But at the end of ten minutes, when the first tentative passages of his playing had passed and it had launched upon a fluent mounting progress, she felt her determination waver. For here was a touch like another that was forever unforgettable—a touch fine and firm and nobly beautiful; and it brought flashing back into Milly's mind things she couldn't bear to remember—Katherine—Phoebe—suggestions of the dreaded *Ghost Piece*. . . . She left the library—sought the company of the twins.

And in the music room Mary, in charmed amazement, watched the fingers and the face of Richard, and listened, deeply still, to his music—to Mozart's music. He seemed quite to have forgotten her—to have forgotten everything. His body, with leaning head, drooped a little, and just perceptibly with the surge and sink of the music it swayed and straightened and relaxed again; the motion of his hands appeared singularly slow, so that they seemed not actually to produce these exquisite passages but only to anticipate and to meet them, not so much to precede as beautifully, perfectly, to accompany them—as though they had been dancers, gliding and stepping, pausing and quickening, upon the shining path of the keyboard; and the music flowed out into the room a facile beauty which seemed not to pass but to linger, to renew itself, to thicken in the air, to cast a spell beneath which all else save the musician's figure, the piano, and that pale stretch of the keyboard, faded into the fringes and the shadows of the scene. . . . But suddenly, with changing face, he stopped—his hands hung still as for a second's listening, and then dropped crashing upon the keys as he whirled about to face, without sight, the curtained entrance to the room.

Mary, at his side in an instant, had seized his arm—"What is it?—Richard—*Richard!*—what *is* it?"

"Please—" his voice trembled—"can we go back? . . . No! not that way! Isn't there another door?"

That last discordant crash, echoing through half the house and falling upon Milly's ear like a signal of disaster, brought her back to the library, half hesitant and atremble with eagerness, to see—always to see—what had happened. She found Mary and Richard, seated so that she couldn't see their faces, already there and talking earnestly. . . . Withdrawing, she took a chair just inside the adjoining room.

She had caught in Richard's voice, even from a distance, the pitch of his agitation; and his words—the last of whatever he had been saying—had sounded as for some profound apology—"I—I don't think I shall ever be able to explain. . . ."

Mary's hand rested upon his arm—"Don't try—don't try. . . . I think I understand anyway. I should have told you before we went into that room that it isn't like the others—like this. You—we—shouldn't have gone . . . but I had no idea it would distress you—really!"

He didn't reply at once; but Milly noticed that his free hand reached to cover that of the girl, which still lay upon his arm. His next speech was quieter—"Well, it's deeply disappointing to me that my—my control of myself—is apparently much less than I had been thinking. . . . But I must say that I'm unable to understand your own self-possession. Do you go in there—into that room—*frequently?*"

"Nearly every day. But," she explained, "my self-possession has nothing to do with it; I'm just less sensitive than you are. I know it's different in there—distinctly different, as you said in the garden the other day; but it could never have been as much so for me as it was just now for you."

He too explained—"It's more than just my sensitiveness, too, I think. . . . It's an abundance in me just now of the quality that makes people afraid. I don't mean," he carefully developed, "that I'm more than normally afraid of physical harm; but I am, tremendously, afraid of the sensation, the feeling, of fear itself!" He paused again, as to look at his thoughts a moment, and when he went on his tone sounded, far better than the words themselves, the dark vividness of his thinking— "When you were a child did they ever put you, for punishment, into a dark closet? Well, they did me—because they couldn't sanction the severity of whippings! . . . They peopled that black little hole with the worst horrors imaginable, and then locked me in it. I can hear the click of that lock yet—and the footsteps growing fainter and fainter—leaving me there alone . . . ! Nothing ever happened, of course; but I used to go nearly mad with the conviction that something would—that I'd see or feel something—that eyes would appear, that fingers would touch me, that things would crawl upon me. The horror of it was too much—too, too great! . . . But what I was afraid of—I see it now—was not so much the eyes or the fingers or the crawling things themselves—not of anything they'd do to me: only that they'd come and *scare* me! It wasn't the horrors I was afraid of; it was the horror. . . . There's no terror on earth like that. I've felt other kinds too, as everyone has, but they're not like this; it's—it's a thing quite by itself . . . one could never forget it.

"Well, it was something very like that that I felt just now in your music room—for all the world as if I were in that closet again—the darkness of this accursed bandage, you know, and then the sense of something—something indefinable, like the great old bogey of my childhood—standing behind me. . . I can't be explicit—one doesn't think! But I *felt*, I say, the presence of something standing just outside those curtains. It was black—about as big as a heavy man or woman; and it was peering in and listening as I played—watching us—watching *me*. . . . It sounds too fantastic, I know, as I describe it; but I assure you it had its effect for me! I—it was necessary—really necessary—for the moment, to escape!"

Mary's eyes had not left his face for minutes, and now that he stopped she had nothing to say. But he must have felt her attention, for after a moment he went on, clearly now as though he found it a comfort to talk, to explain—"And I may as well tell you, since I've got this far, that it was something of the same sort that sent me out into the grounds today. You mentioned, the other day, the 'character' of your room—remember? Well, mine has a character too—only it's not to be called friendly—and it can be, as it was today, insufferable. I don't know that I can describe it better than to say that at its worst it gives me the feeling of being watched—as if the room had another occupant, steadily, silently staring at me. . . . I hardly know what to make of it—of its being as distinct as it is in that one place and its total absence from others. I've explained it in half a dozen ways—attributed it to my imagination, to the fact that my mind's too free to do as it pleases, to being too much alone—for it does seem to be worse since Matthew's begun to disappear. . . . But this is dismal talk, isn't it. Let's change the subject."

After a moment, and with a quietness serious and deliberate, Mary did—"But tell me about Matthew; you didn't finish—"

"Oh. Well, I must say he's still nearly perfect—arranges for all my needs, takes care of me as well as a man could without being actually present. But that's just the difference: he's not present. I'll do him the justice to say he's always on hand at night, when I should have to be alone in my room. . . . I hear him get up sometimes and prowl about and look into the closets and out into the corridor at the most unearthly hours—and I've grown tired of asking him what the matter is. He couldn't be feeling the same way I do—about the room, I mean—for after all Matthew can see. . . . At any rate, it seems impossible to get an explanation out of him."

Mary thought a minute, then asked, "Have you said anything to the doctor—about your feelings? These disturbing ones, I mean. Maybe he ought to know."

Richard shook his head—"I haven't told him, and you mustn't either. I'm ashamed of them, you know—even," he smiled, "—even though I have been unpardonably confidential about them with you."

They did, then, finally change their subject; and Milly, still listening, gave them for a time what attention she could. But Milly didn't, in anything like the degree they seemed to, find her interest ready for what they had now to say; what they had said already—or at least what Richard had said—had gone a bit too deep. So at the end of another fifteen minutes she left her post and quietly, looking a little worried, went off to her room to think.

III

It would take some thinking, conceivably—and would certainly be worth a good deal—to decide for oneself the true significance of the young man's impressions—to make sure whether one wanted to explain them as one somewhat fearfully suspected they could be explained. The house, so far as Milly knew, had been for several years free of anything of the sort that such an explanation must recognize; and Milly, whose experience on that other occasion far back had never failed, on any account of Mary's, as an aid to her conscience, had but too gladly taken this continuance of the general natural condition as half the bargain of which the other half was her own decent discretion. She loved a secret, thrilled to a mystery, delighted in excitement; but Milly's abhorrence of horror was the breadth and depth of her soul; and she wouldn't willingly at this hour, which in all the promise of the association of these children should have been only exquisitely interesting, accept as valid the sign she couldn't nevertheless fail to read into that young man's experience. . . . She ended, at all events, by deciding with what finality she could not to accept it, not to be disturbed by it—to believe instead that Richard had probably "imagined everything" . . . his nerves, of *course*, were not wholly steady; he was unnaturally sensitive, visionary, quick to account for his feelings. . . .

But her first impression nevertheless in a measure persisted, and if the trend of thinking it provoked didn't, after the first few days, frighten her particularly, it did at least tend considerably to sober her—with the result, for one thing, of a change for the better in her attitude toward the children and their beloved attachment. The genuineness of her solicitude deepened. She stopped giggling about them. Where before they had interested her, now they absorbed her. Where before their seclusions had annoyed her, now they filled her with uneasiness. Where before her regard for them had consisted chiefly in the attraction their case held for her as entertainment, it now had the dignity of a kind of apprehensive respect. And these differences made, moreover, for yet others—in particular, for Milly; an improvement in her relations with Mary. The girl, doubtless grateful for the mere cessation of her aunt's teasing, and with the natural good reason of her comparative isolation to appreciate an understanding feminine comradeship, responded to this more serious and seemingly more sensible interest with a fuller, franker kindness than it had in the least entered Milly's head to expect. The improved relation was still, of course, short of what Milly wanted—still yielded nothing to satisfy one's curiosity about the progress of the "romance"—provided not the faintest sign, even, of what the girl thought of her young man's revelation in the library that day. But it nevertheless constituted a better preparation than Milly knew for the understanding they were ultimately to reach. Perhaps, because of her irresistible need to know everything, because of Mary's want of the comfort of another woman's sympathy, because, above all, of the sheer intensity of their common interest, some closer, more dependent confidence was inevitable; in any event, to judge from their evident readiness for the beginning it at last made, it seemed rather definitely to have become at least mutually necessary. . . .

Milly's attention was caught, one morning on Mary's return from an hour in the grounds with Richard, by a shade of sadness in the girl's face. It was not indeed the first time it had been there—not the first time Milly had been perplexed by it; but today it was unquestionably more pronounced, more perplexing, than it had yet been. It was still there—seemed to Milly even to have deepened—at lunch time. And it had not yet passed when at two o'clock, unable longer to silence her curiosity about it, she had come to sit on the edge of Mary's bed in the room beyond the nursery, and to look with an anxious, nervous courage into her niece's face. "Mary," she frankly begged, "tell me what the matter is! What's happened?"

Mary met this with a minute's surprised silence, and then simply, if not with complete finality, answered, "Nothing, Aunty."

"You're worried though—aren't you?—about that young man. . . . Have you quarrelled?"

The earnestness of this brought a smile—"No—we haven't quarrelled."

There was a silence then before Milly spoke again. The girl was too calm, wasn't frank, was concealing something—"I wish you'd tell me, Mary! Maybe I could help you. I want to help you—I want—I want—" and suddenly, astonishingly, Milly burst into tears.

Mary was beside her in an instant, her arm around the bowed shoulders, her smile gone, her own voice grown earnest—"Aunty—please! Don't cry like that. . . ."

"Oh, I know I'm foolish! but I'm so afraid something will happen. . . . I want to know—to know—everything. . . ."

"Well," the girl soothed, "there's no reason you shouldn't. And truly, Aunty, there's nothing serious enough to—"

"Serious enough—!" Milly looked up into her niece's face—"Child, child—it's love isn't it?" She uttered the word as though it were sacred. "And Mary, love—anybody's love—and yours most of all—is serious, to me. I never had any of my own. . . . I—" her eyes filled again—"I'll never have it now, never be able to have it. . . . That, Mary child, is 'serious enough'!" She paused here for a second; but then, because now it seemed impossible to stay the escape of her thoughts—thoughts kept hidden and accumulating for over half her life—she helplessly let them go—"You don't know—God forbid you should ever know!—what it means to face a—an emptiness like that. But I have to! I've faced it every day, every night, for more years than you've lived! It seems that the only thing I can think of, the only thing I ever have thought of, is love—love—a man's love. . . . And you, with your sweet two months of it, know more about it than I ever shall. . . . Do you appreciate that, Mary? Do you know what you have? . . . You're so calm about it! I can't—" and the note of her mystification was deep indeed—"I can't understand that—it seems it ought to mean so much! It's all I ever really hoped for: I haven't sense enough to have hoped for anything else—haven't the capacity to have needed anything more. I've tried, done everything I could—read books, gone to plays and weddings without number—to get a little close to it, been disgraceful and foolish in my interest that I couldn't help—couldn't resist—in the—the better luck of other people. But it never came to *me*. . . . Only now as it comes to you it is nearer to me than ever in my life before—so near that I can see it, feel it, breathe it!—Oh yes, it even has a fragrance . . . but it comes, for me, from so—so far . . ." She choked, and the tears flowed again. Mary held her firmly, and the frizzled little grey-blond head shook on her shoulder—"Please don't hide anything from me, Mary; please tell me; please let me help you, somehow—anyhow. I'll do anything. I'll leave you my money—I could almost give—"

"Oh no, no, Aunty!" The girl's remonstrance was brusque; but her tone, as she went on, grew compassionate enough, and her words sounded honest—"I'm not hiding anything from you, Aunty, really; and I do appreciate it—what I have. Only I can't—can I?—talk about that—what it's like—how it feels? . . . It's too—too much inside—too deep—to come out. Only I'm sure there can be nothing else like it in the world. It makes everything, everybody—especially him—and me—seem . . ." Her voice dwindled suddenly away and colour flooded her face—for she had gone, for Mary, rather far. But she paused only long enough to look down at poor little old Aunt Milly—to look too, perhaps, at the backward stretch of those hopeful and hopeless years of Aunt Milly's poverty—and to select from that coveted abundance which was hers to possess but never to share, some treasure that Aunt Milly might see—might like.

She chose generously; and it detracted not a bit—it even promised something—that she was awkward and visibly hesitant in her offering. It was but a description of a scene—one of those passages Milly had in the past weeks so regretfully missed: they—Richard and Mary—had taken a bench in the grounds near the lifeless fountain, and she had undertaken to make clear for him the reasons for its not playing—"for," as she now told Aunt Milly, "a long time ago, when we had talked about it once, I had half promised him we'd have it repaired, so that when his eyes are well he might see how pretty it is; but afterwards Otis told me it probably would never play again. I wanted Richard," she went on, "to understand about it—and also that I was disappointed; because I'd described it to him and I think—I thought he must be counting on it a little. . . . Well, he didn't answer me for a minute, and I began to think he must not have been listening; and then he said, 'It really won't matter much about the fountain—for won't I have something else to look at?' And I told him yes, of course—lots of things; 'But in particular,' he said; but he didn't say *what* in particular, and—and I didn't ask him. Only I felt I must say something; so I did—the first thing that came into my head—'And then you'll go away, won't you.' And he said, 'Yes—then I'll go away.'

"We didn't say any more then, but just sat there. I was wondering what it would be like when he was gone, and I—I found I didn't like to think about it. . . . After a little while he put his hand on my arm, took hold of my hand—and kissed it—on the fingers first, there, just above the finger-nails, and then here—right there in the palm. I—I can't tell you how I felt, Aunty; I couldn't move—I didn't want to move. . . . I almost cried. Then he said, 'Mary,'—he'd always said Miss Mary before,—and he said—he told me—he—then he told me he loved me—"

The girl stopped, the colour high in her face; and Milly, the tears still glistening on her lashes, gazed entranced at the young face, at the bright young eyes that saw farther than hers would ever see, that shone with something she could but guess the secret of. . . .

Mary resumed—"He told me he knew he shouldn't say it—shouldn't tell me—that I shouldn't listen; that he didn't in the least know what could come of it—what was to become of him—'what sort of man I'll be,' he said, 'when this is over—when this bandage comes off my eyes and I get back into life. . . . For this, just now, isn't life, Mary: it's a kind of Heaven. . . . But tell me—do you mind, are you offended, that I love you?—that I've told you . . . ?'

"And do you know what I did, Aunty?—but I couldn't help it. . . . I kissed him! held his face between my hands and kissed him, kissed him, kissed him. Oh yes, I did that! And then for a long time neither of us said anything; there was nothing to say! But he held me against his side while we sat there. . . . Oh, Aunty, it was lovely—lovely!"

And so too now, Milly and Mary were silent for a long time, and Milly gazed at Mary and Mary seemed to have forgotten her. When they talked again, both were quiet, and Milly, for a queer mixture of gratitude and fear lest the charm be spoilt, the spell be broken, too soon, didn't question. But at last, rising to go—to return to her bedroom and review all this as she wished—she made a venture—"I'm happy for you, my dear—I wish you could know how deeply, deeply happy . . . ! And there wasn't really any cause, this morning, for you to look worried, was there?"

The flush left Mary's face, and her eyes, for the moment just faintly pathetic, and large with a kind of helplessness, met Aunt Milly's—"But he *will* go away, Aunty, when he's well. He mentioned it again just this morning. . . ."

For a second Milly felt too, in her excitement, a check—but only for a second. The lively pleasure, the sweet strong stimulus of this confidence, the resistless promise of developments yet to come, were not now, for Milly, to waver before a mere probability in which she didn't—wouldn't—believe. . . . "Never mind; he won't go. Let me talk to him—"

"But, Aunty—"

"Oh, I'll be careful; I'll not pry! He'll never suspect. . . ."

IV

A few minutes later she had joined him upon a bench in the grounds. He was hatless, and was evidently thinking; and as Milly's quick appraising eye took him in—his fine hair, the visible lines and features of his face, his hands, his clothes—she noticed that the white band across his eyes had been reduced to thinness, and noticed too, in the walk before him, two large irregular scratchings of the initial M—made there doubtless with his now idle stick. She had a smile for this: her subject, quite clearly, should not be difficult to approach.

"I just looked out," she lightly announced—"no, don't get up!—and you seemed so dejected I thought I'd come down and keep you company."

"I'm glad you did." He moved a little to make room for her. "But 'dejected' is a bit strong. . . . 'Contemplative,' I think, would be better."

She accepted the correction—"Oh. Then you were thinking about something pleasant."

"Hardly that," he smiled; "but it was interesting. I was thinking about dreams."

This seemed, to Milly, disappointingly remote—"You might, I should think, have chosen a much more interesting subject than that."

But he wouldn't, just yet, be diverted—"What do you think about them? In general, I mean. . . . Do you believe they are always refashionings of one's own experience—'visualized impressions,' I think they're called, of things that have already happened to us, or that we've desired or seen or heard?"

"I seem to remember something of that kind," she briefly answered, "as one explanation for them."

He nodded. "It seems reasonable enough too, to me; but I dreamed a very simple and vivid—extremely vivid—thing last night, which makes me wonder whether, as an explanation, it's quite complete. You see, there was only one thing in this dream—one person—well, no, really there were two, but one in particular—and that one I'm sure—quite positive—I never saw before. I shouldn't—couldn't—have forgotten her. . . ."

Had he seen Milly's face at this moment, he could hardly have failed to understand that her silence bespoke an interest, for his topic, far less deep than his own. But he could of course see nothing—nothing but the remembered, the evidently absorbing, objects of his vision—"You know, there are moments when I doubt its having been a dream at all . . . but of course it must have been. I awoke, or dreamed that I did, with the feeling that somebody else was in my room. You know the feeling of having someone stare at you? Well, it was like that. And without thinking, I slipped my bandage off again—the doctor had had it off during the afternoon. The first thing I saw was the light: Matthew had a candle burning; then I made him out asleep on his cot; and then I saw my lady. She was sitting in the rocking chair—an elderly lady, quite heavy, wearing a woollen bath robe—and her hands were working rapidly at something. I couldn't see anything in them; but she made motions like a woman knitting—and from the speed of her hands I should think she must have been extraordinarily skilful. . . ."

Milly's inattention, her small annoyance, had vanished; her narrowed eyes were fixed, half scared, upon his face; and if she still wished not to hear any more of this, it was now for another reason indeed—a reason which held her silent, fascinated, as he continued—"I watched her, I should say, for thirty seconds before she looked up so that I could see her face. . . . And I assure you, Miss Milly, I never saw that face before! It was dark, all dark—even to the whites of her eyes—like old paper; and the flesh—particularly in the cheeks—was loose and hanging. She looked weary—extremely, unutterably tired. . . . I remember she had two moles on one cheek, too, and a moustache and heavy eyebrows. But her eyes struck me, I think, more than anything else. They were brown—the kind that look hot—and they had a certain steadiness, and there was an expression in them that was meant, distinctly, for me. I won't say it was evil; it was—well, just intently contemplative—as though she had been trying to decide upon what she should do about me—or to me. It seemed clear enough that she intended to do something; the promise of that was not a bit less there because she was undecided. In fact it's that—that rather sinister promise—that was so vivid. It struck me with a distinct shock. Two months ago, if I had encountered that . . ." He left this unfinished; and Milly, with blanched face, sat now rigidly erect, still speechless, staring at his unconscious calmness as though it had been a horror. He waited for some seconds, jabbing quietly now with his stick an ever deepening hole in the ground between his feet; then, a little absently, he asked, "What do you think of it?"

Milly could but stammer an answering question—"But—but that isn't all! What else happened? . . . How did it end?"

"That's not very clear now—not nearly so clear as the rest. But I remember the door was open (it was warm, and I suppose Matthew hadn't closed it) and I was suddenly aware of another woman standing there—just outside, in the corridor. I don't know why she didn't come in; I felt that she wanted to. But she didn't look at me; she was watching my other lady; and she—the one in the chair—turned around to meet the look. Have you ever seen people try to stare each other down?

Well, that's what those two seemed to be doing; and the one in the hallway got the better of it. There was a tension in it even for me—I recall that; I'd have said my ladies were enemies—at least the face I could see—the dark one—had hatred in it for the other—black hatred, that looked futile somehow, too. But her eyes dropped first and looked away—not at me this time, though, but back down at her hands, which went to work again upon something I couldn't see. I'm sure it must have been knitting—would have been knitting if it had been anything.

"That's all. It had begun to feel—while she had her eyes on me—like a nightmare; I think I'd have waked up yelling before very long. But it must have ended peacefully: the next thing I remember Matthew was straightening my bedclothes and muttering about something. . . ."

He stopped here, waiting, apparently, for her comment. But she had none—had, intensely, almost tremblingly quiet now, another question—"And what—what did the other woman look like—the one who didn't come in?"

"I couldn't see her very well; but she was tall, wore something white, and had a beautiful head of hair. . . . But," he smiled now with his insistence, "you haven't said what you think about it—about the failure of the psychology-book's explanation."

Getting to her feet, stifling some hysterical urge to say, to do, she knew not what, Milly stammered out—"I—I can't!—I haven't time now. . . . I just remembered something . . ."—and, leaving Richard to resume after a moment his gentle jabbing of the garden walk, she ran off to the house, to her room—to think—with her mind, her memory, her imagination, full as they had not been full for years, of the grim and hateful visage of Phoebe. . . .

Before what she conceived as the necessity for some immediate saving action, her agitation, after twenty minutes in the stillness of her room, had in some measure passed—had passed, at any rate, sufficiently to leave her capable of something like clear thinking. She had been quick enough to interpret what Richard had just described—interpret it for him, for Mary, above all for this lovely "romance" in which she had just begun to share—as a presage of disaster; and her fear-quickened little mind could see but one fact else—that they must escape it! He mustn't, she saw with unanswerable conviction, stay in that room another night—must not, if it could in any way be helped, even so much as enter it again—ever again! Phoebe would probably—would *surely*—come back; and though the return were to amount to nothing more than a repetition of last night's experience, just suppose he were to realize what that in itself amounted to . . . ! It was clear—startlingly, chillingly clear to Milly, who knew fear quite as well as did Richard—what that might mean . . . !

Her decision was hardly formed when, startled by a knock at her door, she opened it to look into the inquiring eyes of Mary. For a second Milly could merely awakeningly look at her. Then—"Oh, I'm sorry, my dear; I wasn't able to talk about it. . . . Something else. . . . I met the doctor; and Mary, Richard must have another room. The doctor wants him to have another room—where the light is better." Pausing only long enough to fix it in her mind that she must see the doctor—see him, without fail, *first*—tomorrow, she then hurried on—"It's still quite early, and I think we could—the doctor wants him moved at once. . . . If you'll send for Otis, I'll go tell the twins. I haven't seen them yet; and the doctor didn't have time to wait. Even Richard doesn't know about it. . . ."

She fairly pushed Mary into the corridor, towards the staircase; and there Mary, stopping for a short frank laugh at Aunt Milly's excitement, detained her for a detail—"Which room is he to have?"

"Oh thank Heaven there are rooms enough! It really doesn't matter." But then, with a thought for something else, Milly's eyes softened for a second, and her hand sought Mary's—"Wouldn't it be nice if he had yours?"

Mary coloured—"Well, it's the nicest room in the house. I think he'd like it."

"He'd love it!" Milly kissed her, recalled her purpose, and hurried off, calling back over her shoulder—"Besides, Matthew could use the nursery."

(But, as happened, Matthew wasn't to use it long. Mary informed her aunts that same evening that he was, at his own urgent but unexplained request, to give up his service with Richard.)

*   *   *

If Milly's determination, and yet more the decisive accomplishment of it with which the remainder of this day was filled, were largely the issues of apprehension, they were at once hardly less also the issues of elation. Mary's confidence, this stimulating sense of usefulness, this delicious participation, made, quite apart from the effect of her fears, a tremendous difference—filled her with reckless gratitude toward Mary, with a courage that warmed like wine—lightened her step, flushed her face, brightened her very eyes. . . . But, for this high excited confidence, there fell upon her, in the dusk of the day, a damper, a decisive touch of restraint. She had looked in for the last time on Richard, now in the nursery, had tripped thence down the corridor, had glanced at the door of Phoebe's now vacant room, which stood a few inches open, and had stopped. Before today it would have been difficult to entice Milly into that room; less yet would she have been likely to go in voluntarily and alone. But on an impulse—the brave issue, for Milly, of her mood, of her success—she went in now—though a little timidly even yet, and but just across the threshold. It was perhaps well that she did—perhaps altogether best that her check, sharp and cogent as it was, should have been brought about just now, fortuitously at first. It came, at any rate, swiftly, chillingly, warningly, and all simply as a flash of thought—the sudden realization, excluding, for the moment, everything else from her mind, that she had *opposed Phoebe*. . . . Her satisfaction, her enthusiasm, her new courage, fell to nothing. If the walls had suddenly contracted upon her they could hardly have crushed more definitely against her body than did that thought upon her consciousness. Phoebe's bed, Phoebe's wash-stand, Phoebe's wardrobe, Phoebe's rocking chair in the far dim corner, everything, confusedly and all at once fairly cried it out at her that the action of this afternoon, her satisfaction in it, her anticipations, her emotions, her intentions, conspicuously, glaringly, swelled the measure of her defiance of the wish and the will of Phoebe. . . . Milly pressed her hands over her ears and backed out into the corridor, and thence, pale and scared, she hurried downstairs to the dining room—where the others were.

V

She thought a good deal, on that evening and for days afterward, about those few minutes—about all that had happened—about all that might happen—above all, about Phoebe. Not of course that she liked to think about Phoebe: Milly frankly didn't consider her old sister, in any light, because she liked to; and she only searchingly considered her now in every light, because, to account for what she had heard, and yet more for what she feared, she could do no less. What she wanted—indeed, needed—was some notion of what was to be expected of Phoebe with regard to Richard and Mary; and she found, in the queer consistency of her reasoning, that the answer to that question was not, as had at first appeared, a little darkly obvious, but was first dependent upon the answer to that other question of what, on the same ground, was to be expected of Katherine!

Her memory of what had passed, years before, between the two women was still sufficiently vivid to leave little doubt as to where they must stand with relation to each other; and it seemed clear enough, too, that the manner, if not the method, of Katherine's dealing with Phoebe in those last unforgettable hours was but the logical manner for Phoebe to have dealt, since then, with Mary. Didn't it follow, then, since Mary hadn't been dealt with in any fatal manner whatever, that her mother's old score with Phoebe was yet unsettled?—that Phoebe's hatred and Katherine's single vulnerability in the person of her daughter had made unchangingly all these years—made still—for the perpetuation of their contention? Given Phoebe's interest and Phoebe's character, what else was one to think? . . . Poor Milly could think nothing else; and, as her conception of that contention broadened and darkened, could but stare into it in scared wonder—to shudder a little at what she couldn't help making of its magnitude, its pitch and tension, its ceaseless inscrutable play of forces. . . . The details of its processes she perforce left alone— they were not for her; she could at best but think of those two, invisible, inseparable, trailing through the rooms and corridors of the house, the one watching, watching, watching as only she could, the other calmly, imperiously restraining as only she could. They must have been at it un-ceasingly—through Mary's childhood, day and night, every hour, every minute—must have hovered over her at meals, at work, at play—must have watched her leave the house and return to it—must have followed her at every step—have known every act, every word, every joy and sad-ness and secret through half the child's life. . . .

There was still, of course, the comforting evidence of Mary's healthy happy presence to indicate that, so far, Katherine had proved the stronger. But Milly couldn't over-value that; for hadn't the terms of the conflict now distinctly changed? Hadn't they, for Katherine, plainly stiffened? Wouldn't Phoebe, divining the relation of the children, have by now also seen that an affliction visited upon Richard would be, for the effect she sought, second only to one visited upon Mary herself? And could Katherine always be as successful in shielding him as she had been in shielding Mary? Didn't that dream—that experience—of Rich-ard's prove, and wasn't it the significance of what she had heretofore considered merely fantastic notions in her young friends about the characteristic peculiarities of some of the rooms, that there were places to which Katherine, not less than Phoebe herself, didn't—perhaps couldn't—go, and, consequently, couldn't act? . . . They seemed, in-deed, as Milly intently worked it out, to walk nowhere now that they hadn't familiarly walked in life—so that Katherine had remained in the corridor on that night of Richard's visitation simply because she must; the library, the grounds, Mary's bedroom, with their friendliness, had been familiar to Katherine but never, as Milly remembered, to Phoebe; and if the happier air of these places spoke for the absence of her old sister, surely the mixed mood of the music room, the distress of Richard on the day he had played there, must be taken as speaking not less, on the other hand, for her presence!

But if her deductions seemed up to this point sufficiently sound, Milly could at last but too clearly see that they didn't, on the score of what was to be expected of the future, help very much—that they yielded as good as no measure at all of Richard's jeopardy, of Mary's immunity, of her own responsibility! . . . There was no help for it—she could go, simply, no further. And so, still fearfully wondering—and taking pains to make no further flagrant display, inside the house, of her own allegiance—she could for the moment but uneasily wait. . . .

*   *   *

On the day of Matthew's departure she waylaid him outside the gate to question him for whatever she could learn, for reassurance or further fearful inference, about his reason for leaving. She got no more out of him than had Richard; but from something about him—his polite stubbornness, his evasions and the way he looked—Milly divined that he was afraid—must be leaving the house because he was afraid to stay longer in it. This conviction stopped her questions: it was all—it was even in a sense more than—she wanted; but she kept him a moment more, to ask him, this time, to get for her the key to Phoebe's room. On this, his pale little eyes looked steadily and with sufficient understanding into her own—"And shall I lock the door?"

"Yes! Be sure it can't be opened from the outside! And please don't give me the key in the house; don't speak of it there. . . . Couldn't you get it now, and bring it to me here? I'll wait."

She had to wait longer than it should have taken him—allowing even for a reasonable hesitation before the door; and when at last he did return it was to state gravely and as for a recognizable significance—"The key is gone."

"And the door—?"

"Unlocked and standing open. I closed it."

She had later too, in the grounds, a chat with the doctor, in the midst of which he announced, to her consternation, that Richard's bandage was soon to be replaced by glasses. The boy was eager for the change—unusually eager, said the doctor—and apparently for some very special reason: there was something, or somebody, he was sure, that his patient particularly wanted to have a look at—

"—But you said," interposed Milly, her words tumbling out headlong—"you said that he'd had some nervous trouble—before. Is he

quite over that, do you think, too? That is, isn't he unusually susceptible to impressions—to fear, especially? And if he were to—to be startled or something—frightened—wouldn't that be dangerous for him?"

The doctor met this with a silent calm scrutiny of her face; and
when he replied it was not with answers but with questions of his own.
Milly was glad enough to answer him, to unburden her mind, to explain
her concern; and she was grateful to feel him take in attentively,
gravely, quite everything she had to say. She wondered a little that
some of it didn't surprise him, seemed even familiar to him; but she
thought she understood that well enough when, after a few minutes, he
let drop that he had had recently a call from Matthew. Her own eyes
opened a little for this—for that voluntary act of the little man who just
the other day had confronted her with his understanding and significant look and his failure to find Phoebe's key; but she was not too surprised to fail at once devoutly to bless him for it. For Milly saw it as
support—important support, she thought—for the case which, out of
her fears, her convictions, her sympathies, she felt it imperative on this
short notice to make with the doctor. The thought of Richard walking
abroad in the house with full sight had already, in twenty minutes, filled
her with forebodings; and, so far from concealing them from her lis-
tener, she strove with all the eloquence she could command to make
him share them. She couldn't tell, from his impassive face, what he was
thinking of her, of her appeal, of her arguments, of the prodigious thing
she was trying to make him believe; but when she had finished, had
poured into his attention everything at all to her purpose she could
think of, he did look for a silent second as though he were impressed,
and his reply at least didn't contradict or discredit—

"It might appear, then, that your fine old house holds not only precisely what's best in the world for him, but precisely what's worst as
well."

"Yes—yes. And it doesn't matter really whether there *is* anything
horrible or not, does it? It's enough—would be enough, I mean—if he
only got to thinking, only feared, that there was.... He mustn't have
any such notions as that, must he? And I think, if he can't see, that he
won't guess, won't know!"

The doctor thought. "We might take him away altogether."

Milly hadn't expected this—"But—but do you think he'd go—?"

"—and leave his lady?" concluded the doctor. They appeared, looking into each other's eyes, to weigh this for a minute. "I wonder," he at
last quietly said, "if he expects to marry her. Do you know how they
stand on that?"

Milly shook her head. "There's no question about Mary. But isn't it possible he might not ask her? I've an idea he considers himself something of an invalid—thinks, maybe, he might prove troublesome—a burden—"

"Nonsense—absolute nonsense!" The doctor rose to go—"I'll straighten him out on that!"

VI

Meanwhile the relation of Richard and Mary had of course come clearly enough to be recognized for what it was by everybody in the house; and Mary had faced a thorough questioning by the twins and listened to three lectures on the subject of proper conduct for young ladies. The important result of their awakening was, however, as the girl later reported to Milly, that they "didn't object so *very* much, bless their hearts!" and indeed the only visible difference it made was that Richard and Mary met henceforth less often in the grounds alone and more often under the old ladies' eyes in the parlour. Milly, of course, disapproved of even so small a limitation as that—but, because it fell in for the moment conveniently with a plan she had for a bit of pleasure for her young friends, she didn't, just yet, complain of it.

This plan, which she had carried in secret since the great day of Mary's confidence, blossomed quite perfectly. One evening after an hour's watching of the quiet group in the parlour, Milly proposed, since it was a lovely evening, that they go into the grounds and enjoy it. She foresaw of course that the twins wouldn't, that the children would, and that her own chaperonage would count for something against her sisters' scruples. . . .

Outside, walking fast and well in front, she led them towards the west side of the house, and turned upon them, on reaching the corner, an elated, eager face—"I—I've made you a present!" Mary, coming abreast of her, halted for sheer delighted surprise; sightless Richard, with a swift smile, asked, "Do I—*don't* I—hear the fountain? . . ." and a little later, when they stood grouped near it, they watching, he listening, he thanked her: "It's truly a present, Miss Milly, for me. It makes these grounds quite—quite perfect."

And indeed for that hour they seemed to be—perfect for cool stillness, for peace, for the night's light which lay upon them with a heavenly softness. . . . The trees—great towers of shadow—slept soundless; the air and the life of the earth were still; and the fountain, set like a jewel in the green-black expanse of the lawn which spread away into the dark, lifted its spray like a curtain of silk and silver, let fall its drops like a rain of pearls. . . .

Milly wandered away; and Richard and Mary seated themselves in the deep dusk of the garden's edge. For a long time they were silent; speech, under the spell of this peace, of their nearness and their touch, could have meant little. . . .

His first words were for Milly and her fountain—"Do you suppose she did do it, as she said, for us?"

Her answer, dropping like an added quietness, sufficiently explained—"Yes . . . she likes us, you know."

For softness, for simple, gentle gravity, his response quite matched her own—"I seem to feel that she loves us. . . . Not so much, though, as individuals but as—as what we represent together—above all, as what we should represent—together." He reached up, to hold her cheek against his face—"Do you love me?"

"Yes, Richard."

"And would you—*will* you marry me?"

For answer she took his face in her hands, as she had done on another occasion, and looked at him—at his forehead, his hair that was like finest silk, his nose and mouth and chin—as much of his face as she could see. . . . Her lips all but trembled as she answered—"Yes, yes, yes, Richard—only—Oh, don't you know?—there is the condition—" She didn't, perhaps couldn't, finish—could, for some exquisite, inexpressible intensity of ecstasy and doubt, but speechlessly, hungrily hold his face between her hands.

"Condition—?" The question was large indeed for Richard.

"Suppose"—her voice trembled—"suppose you don't like me—after you see me . . . ?"

His hands found her shoulders in an instant, drew her against him—"If that's the condition . . ." For him, certainly, it was already settled—"Mary, will you marry me?"

For all answer this time she kissed him, kissed his insistence to silence, and then, standing, looked away from him—looked at Milly's fountain, at the trees, the sky, the far, far distant dust of the stars. And thus standing, lighted by starlight that showed but half distinctly her slim straight stature, that left half in shadow her head and face, her neck and arms and the whole fine firmness of her body—thus for the first time Richard saw her. And thus sitting, gazing at her with his adoration and an attention much like wonder in his face, Mary turned after a few seconds and also for the first time truly saw Richard. Her first act after the short surprised gasp was for his eyes—was swiftly to cover them with her own hands—"Richard—your eyes!"

"There's no danger—really—see, it's dark. . . . Really, Mary. . . ." And he held her hands away and drew her towards him and downward so that at last she knelt, and they looked long and intently into each other's face—a look tender, searching, anxious, in which mingled appraisal and adoration—the look of the lovers they were, and still hardly less of the strangers they couldn't help being. . . . "And now that you've seen me, and I've seen you and love you more than ever—love you above anything on earth—love you so that I fairly ache with it—Mary, will you marry me?"

"Yes, Richard."

*   *   *

When they returned to the house—still alone, for Milly hadn't rejoined them—he wore again his bandage, so that as they closed the great door behind them he was again safely blind.

And back in the grounds, a few yards from the bench on which they had sat and breathed and murmured and caressed each other full of their rapture, sat Milly, weeping. The poor little lady had not, at first, intended to spy and listen; but such an occasion was not for Milly to resist. This was the stuff, truly, of which her dreams were made: she had dreamed, had planned, this hour—had set the stage, had placed the actors in it, and had found it, simply, impossible not to stay and view the scene. Well, she had viewed it—had seen the play of tenderness, had heard the utterances, had watched the faces, of lovers at love; and Milly's cup was full. Her sobs—silent, shuddering sobs—continued long after her children had gone in, and when she arose at last and entered the house, it was dark and still with sleep.

VII

But as the door closed at her back and she faced the lightless silence within, her emotion of the last hour thinned—vanished . . . the memory of Phoebe, sudden, unaccountable, vivid, flooded her mind; and there descended upon her chillingly, like an icy wind, a sense as of near invisible movement—of action—of conflict, vital and somewhere close— conflict hidden and soundless but yet with an echo—a sure echo, for Milly, of mounting horror. . . . Groping, she found the wall switch, flooded the hall and stairs with light—swept the space with wide eyes— saw nothing . . . saw nothing, of course! because here necessarily there would *be* nothing. But upstairs, where the children were . . . If her sense were right there was assuredly something there: a danger—and a danger for them! She climbed the stairs, reached the top trembling and whimpering, and, half-blind with tears, faced down the corridor: not toward that wing in which lay her own room, but the other—the one holding the rooms of Richard and of Phoebe. . . .

The corridor was dark—a shaft of blackness, at whose end lay the nursery, and beyond that Richard's bedroom. She gazed a minute motionless, seeing nothing; and then, suddenly, she did see—saw the nursery door open, saw Richard framed in the light from within, saw him, eyes unbound, step into the corridor. About midway between them stood Phoebe's door; and Milly, running towards him, reached it first, passed it before he had come yet half way. He had, on seeing her, halted abruptly, and had raised for the moment one hand to cover his eyes. She didn't notice at once that he carried something in the other—"Mr. Richard—what is it—what is it?"

He looked at her then and she saw that his eyes, about which she had wondered, were dark and beautiful; but traces of the start she had given him were still visible in his face—"You must pardon me, Miss Milly. I—I didn't recognize—didn't expect to see anybody. . . . I was startled—"

"Yes, I know; but you shouldn't be here—that is—without your bandage. I'm afraid—for your eyes. Please don't strain them—please—"

"Oh," he could be easy about that—"they'll stand this—this light—very well, I assure you; they're being exposed every day—"

"Yes, but—forgive me; I'm a cranky old maid—you know you should be asleep; it's one o'clock in the morning!"

He smiled. "I know. I've been in bed, but was restless. I thought if I got up for a little it might help—that nobody would be disturbed if I just walked up and down this hallway a little. Besides," he went on, "I must return this." And he held up Phoebe's key—"I found it on the floor of the nursery room just tonight." While she stared at it he covered his eyes again and went calmly on—"You know, when your sisters asked me if I had it I was quite sure I hadn't. Matthew said we'd left it, on its chain, inside its rightful door. We'd never used it. I wonder what made him take it off. . . . But I can return it now; and anyway, you know, I've always wanted to have a look at that room."

"No—you mustn't—you *mustn't*!" Poor Milly's emphasis—she was near to tears—clearly surprised him—"the room is—is occupied—now!"

"Occupied?"

"Yes—yes—occupied—by a woman."

"Oh. . . . Well," he smiled, "it *is* fortunate you caught me."

"Yes," Milly developed; "it's a friend of Mrs. Stroub's—the house-keeper; we let her have it for a short time . . . but—but,"—she prayed for courage—"*I'll* take the key if you like; I—I can give it to her." And as she took it from his hand her heart first gave a bound for the relief of knowing him to be without it, and then stood still for the horror of having it herself.

He thanked her, and then, a little as if at a loss for something else to say, remarked that this was his second occasion on this night for gratitude—that his feeling about what she had done with the fountain—! She interrupted him, took his arm and turned him back towards the nursery—"But I'm still very anxious about you. Won't you go back to bed—cover your eyes again? If you're really so grateful, as you said just now, about the fountain, you could repay me—"

They had reached the door and he held it open for her to go in—"How—repay you? I'll be glad indeed—"

"Then don't ever go walking about like this again without your eye-bandage. That's simple, isn't it? . . . It's all I ask of you. It really isn't much, is it?" Her voice fairly pleaded.

"It's odd," he noted; "Mary asked the same thing of me tonight."

"And you shouldn't *shouldn't* have disobeyed!"

"I shan't again," he smiled; "I promise you both. But I assure you you're over-cautious for me. . . . I wonder," he abruptly shifted his subject, "if it would be unfair to tell you—before she has an opportunity—that she made *me* a promise too, to-night—to marry me."

Milly's eyes dropped—rested on the key still grasped in her hand—and then filled with tears—"Well, I'm very happy for you—for you both. I—I'm sure—I'm sure. . . . Oh, but I'm so afraid something might happen. . . . It—it would break my heart!"

Under his kind smile she stood a moment frankly crying, still clutching Phoebe's key, and then turned to leave the nursery. But, laying his hands on her shoulders, he stopped her and looked a minute deep, deep into her queer little face; and Milly, trembling and flushing under his touch, raised her red-rimmed wet pale eyes to meet his look. . . .

The next minute she was in the corridor, running its length towards her bedroom; and her heart pounded, her eyes saw nothing, and the hard sweetness of a young man's kiss burned hot upon her mouth.

*   *   *

But Milly's night was not yet done: even before she had gained her room the turbulent little ecstasy set stirring by that kiss—that first masculine kiss—had passed for something far less sweet. The difference, flashing upon her at a particular instant of her headlong flight, had at first consisted of hardly more than a vivid sudden awareness of Phoebe's door; but it had been enough to check Milly's breath, to make her choke and falter; and two seconds later, facing her mirror with wide scared eyes, her joy went cold as she took the measure of what, within thirty minutes, she had done—of what Phoebe must know she had done! The features of her action were few enough—the interception of Richard on his way to Phoebe's room, the lie about its occupancy, the insistent warning and the promise extracted about his eyes—but their consequence might be terrible! . . . Suppose she were to see Phoebe— just *see* her—as Richard had, sometime in the middle of the night . . . or meet her, maybe, somewhere in the corridors or rooms of the house! Suppose Phoebe were to abandon Richard and Mary and undertake only to punish *her!* Perhaps even now the dreaded figure stood outside her door, waiting—waiting! . . . Possibilities crowded pell-mell into her mind, lifting irresistibly the pitch of her terror. At one instant she foresaw an issue quick and fatal, at another a prolonged and harrowing agony; but whatever the detail, it pointed, for herself, disaster. The thought of Katherine, whose understanding she took for granted quite as readily as she took Phoebe's, yielded scant comfort. She recalled too clearly her own old score with Mary's mother, saw too plainly how easily now Katherine's protection might stop with the children—might, for all she knew, be insufficient even for them, since they were two. . . .

Meantime, there, in her hand, was the key. . . . Tomorrow or the next day or next week, Richard would tell Mary about it, about his midnight talk with Aunt Milly—would discover that she had lied about the room. They would wonder about that—perhaps laugh a little; and perhaps one of them, or both, would just open Phoebe's door—just go in. . . . Go in—! Milly's thought stopped, fixed upon that possibility; and after some seconds—after her turbid little soul had grown calm and her heart like a piece of ice—she opened her door and stepped into the corridor.

Two doors down was Mary's room; a little farther, over the head of the stairs, burned a faint light; and beyond—steps and steps beyond— stood Phoebe's door.

Milly moved towards it, got as far as the light, faltered—stopped. Her muscles quivered, her legs shook, she hardly breathed—but she didn't know; all she knew, all she could think, was that henceforth down that hall she shouldn't walk alone. So, in order not to see what went with her, she shut her eyes, shut them tight; and as she crept forward again the prayer in her heart was not to God but to Katherine.

All now was black—black and blank, but for the sensations of the hand that felt her progress along the wall. It passed first across the door of an empty room, told her next that she had reached the locked and haunted chamber of her ancestor, paused at last on the frame of Phoebe's door—touched gently the door itself, and felt it yield! It was open. . . .

The blackness, of a sudden, was intolerably heavy—too, too heavy—and she sank to her knees. But courageously, valiantly, she didn't let go . . . it was only necessary to find the door-knob. . . . But that reach must carry her hand, half her arm, *into* the room! She waited—opened her eyes a hair's breadth—saw, or thought she saw, the door move a little, move towards her. It came nearer—lacked but a few inches—retreated a little—moved forward again—and she seized it, fiercely held it shut, locked it, got to her feet, and fled.

* * *

Next morning, pale and a little grim, she appeared at breakfast in street clothes. But she was not going out; her errand was already done. She hadn't slept—though there had been, immediately following her return from Phoebe's door, a long lapse in which she had lain huddled in the centre of her bed, motionless, sightless, without sensation, without thought. And afterward, when that numbness had passed, the first thing that happened in her brain was the birth of an idea of escape: it would, she seemed to see, be a very simple matter . . . merely pack a few things, go away—leave this horrid place—not come back, ever. . . . She sat upright, decided to do it! Now! And she changed her dress—wondering, as she snapped its fastenings at her hip, if this one would be appropriate for travel; for of course she would travel. What did people take, travelling? Underclothing? Handkerchiefs? . . . But she had no travelling bag—never had needed such a thing. Well, she'd buy one in the morning, and buy what she needed to put into it too; the shop-people would know, would help her. . . . Idle handed then, she began to wonder where she should go—what she should do; and a suddenly looming view of how alone she should be, out there in a world she knew nothing about, scared her afresh. . . . And what of the twins—of the children? Why, the children were to be married—there would be a wedding! How could she go away, after all? If she did, she should miss everything—forfeit her own sweet share in the thing for which she had so deeply yearned—miss her part in its preparation, lose all the pleasure. . . .

With the coming of daylight her fear lost a little its edge; and she changed her mind—decided against going in any case until after the wedding. Meantime of course—and she meant this this time!—she would be cautious, extremely cautious—would provoke nothing; and maybe—God grant it!—nothing would happen. . . . She tried only half successfully not to recognize it as a violation of that caution that she sneaked out of the house a short time later with a plan already formed to lose, irrecoverably, Phoebe's key. She didn't carry it, of course— conspicuously carried nothing in her hands; and it was only to be hoped that the three thicknesses of clothing, beneath which she could feel it unmistakably enough against her flesh, would sufficiently hide it!

*   *   *

Henceforth for a time she was seriously consistent, in as many ways as she could be, in observing that determination to be careful. Particularly she guarded her speech, even though now the subject of the wedding was on every tongue in the house. She avoided certain parts of the house, notably the music room, the upstairs wing that held Richard's and Phoebe's rooms—moved about where she must looking always downward, so as to see only the floors—spent hours away from the house and in the grounds—scurried off to her bedroom before dark. And there she thought long and deeply, worried greatly, made her will, looked out upon the grounds, cried a good deal. . . . And the wrinkles deepened in her face; she forgot details of her customarily elaborate toilette, and frequently appeared yellow and pitifully ugly; even her clothes lost for a time their neatness, seemed to hang badly, showed spots. . . .

But as time passed and nothing unnatural, nothing in the least horrible, occurred, her caution lapsed into something like habit, she lost by degrees her unprecedented gravity, her thoughts returned again irresistibly to her young friends—to the wedding. And yet later, with her interest and the activity she found for herself in the preparations, she forgot altogether, at moments, to be afraid, to be careful—grew even a little bold, made free of the house again. . . . She tripped out with Mary to shop, and bought "things" for her whose fineness fairly took the girl's breath; she spent hours with her over the trousseau, and the store of her information must have struck wonder in Mary's mind even while some of her comment brought blushes into Mary's face. She was generous to lavishness; she knew from long, long observation what was best; and her girl—and her boy—were to have just that—the best. It might have seemed less their wedding than her own; certainly she let herself go in its preparation hardly less far than she could have done if it had been her own.

For after all—and in spite, even, of the lurking shadow of her fear—this was the best passage of Milly's life—the sort of thing, simply, for which she hungrily, pathetically, tragically lived. She loved it—deeply, genuinely loved it—loved the children—loved above all their love, whose beginning she had been first to appreciate, for whose growth she had trembled, for whose beauty she had wept in sheer tumultuous rapture that night before her fountain, for whose aid she had poured forth her encouragement, her money, even a measure of courage which nothing else, assuredly, could ever have evoked! She couldn't help it: it was simply natural—as natural as that on the day of the wedding she should rise from a bed sleepless for conscious dreaming, that she should waken the house, that later she should demand the privilege of dressing the bride, and that at last, as she looked on the vision of loveliness that Mary was, she should forget even to be afraid.

It was, the day, all beautiful: the old guests who came, the doctor, the twins in handsome new gowns, and in tears—Richard, and Mary above all. . . .

VIII

The house, late in the evening, was at last quite still. Because the train which was to carry the children away didn't leave until morning, and because by Richard's desire they were to spend their night here—in their beloved nursery bedroom—the twins had decided they should have the complete vast privacy of the house, and had accordingly—determinedly, tearfully, handsomely, and taking Milly with them—gone away. The farewells were over, for the departure was to take place too early to disturb the old ladies because of it, and Richard and Mary, flushed and bright-eyed and serious and delicate, had been but a few minutes alone in the room which now was doubly theirs.

He had, in the dim light, but just wonderingly surveyed it—taken in its adornment of ribbon and flowers, linen and silk—caught sight for the first time of a gift—"Is this magic? Somebody has been here since I—"

"Oh," she readily explained, "Aunt Milly of course. Hasn't she been wonderful?"

"Well, next to you—"

"She's responsible even for me—and you told me yourself I was lovely." Mary looked down at her dress—"But you've mussed me terribly!"

Richard smiled. "No amount of generosity, though, could make her—could make anybody—responsible for the loveliness I was talking about; and no amount of mussing could spoil it. Because, you see, it has nothing to do with dresses—it would be the same loveliness in one as in another!"

Without speech, Mary thanked him; and after a little he continued—"But Aunt Milly has been wonderful. It looks—" he glanced over the room again—"it looks as if she might even have understood why I wished to—wished for us to stay here tonight."

Mary, who had seen Aunt Milly's face when she learned of that wish, might have doubted this; but she said nothing, and he quietly went on—

"You know, it was mostly because I wanted to realize a little notion I've had about your—your presence here. It has seemed to me, ever so positively, that you've never wholly been out of the room since I came into it. It's extraordinary, I know, but it's quite the truth. I've thought with you, talked with you, dreamed with you, every day and every night since they moved me here. The peace of it, the loveliness you couldn't help filling it with, the feeling that you were—well, here, with me, all the time, were almost as vivid as this very reality of having you. And I wanted this—these few hours of the reality—to crown those many others. Nothing else could; no other place would have done as well, could have been quite the same. And I knew you'd know it, too, and be glad about it; for you told me yourself—remember?—about this room—that it was the happiest of all the house."

Mary, quietly enough, could answer that—"But I didn't say that at all because it had been mine. All these rooms have something about them like—like spirits of their own; and this one, this room, had been my wonderful mother's."

He answered this after a moment quite as seriously as she had uttered it—"And that, of course—because your mother loved you—might account for its friendliness for you, but not for me. How could that—what it meant for you on her account—have reached me?"

She met his smile, which was grave and kind—"I'm old-fashioned enough to believe that perhaps it's because she loves you too; and more than that—as you said about Aunt Milly that night—that she loves 'us.'"

"Well," he answered, "I'll be old-fashioned too, for anything so beautiful as that. . . ." He had been standing before her, and now, taking her hands, he raised her, held her—"I'd like to believe it, Mary. It's as if, as a kind of final touch, it were a last beauty to bless what we have and what this means for us—as if we had gained even the sanction of angels. . . . That makes it—doesn't it?—complete."

"Yes, Richard—complete . . . complete. . . ."

*   *   *

Elsewhere the house slept; and from outside, to the solitary watcher in the grounds, it towered in the dark still and shapeless and wholly black but for the faintly lighted rectangles of that chamber's windows. For Milly had come back, and had sat there concealed for a long time watching those windows, thrilling to the passage of shadows across them, wondering—wondering—forgetful, in the spell of her thoughts, of everything but that room—its occupants. And when at last the light disappeared and darkness closed over the windows, she stayed on, her face still lifted towards them, still thinking—still intently, agitatedly thinking. After a time, however, she arose and made her way, a little undecidedly, to the door of the house. But here she hesitated, recalling that she had determined not to go in, telling herself with what emphasis she could that it wasn't right, that it would be futile—above all, that it might be unsafe! . . .

When she reached the head of the stairs she stopped again. And the unheeded self-dissuasion that had run through her brain as she crept through the lower hall and up the steps quite suddenly ceased; and with it everything else in her mind—thought, memory, sense—seemed to die and drop away: everything save only those two passions which she could never wholly lose and which surged up now irresistibly to possess her, to hold her for seconds facing down that corridor, irresolute, reasonless, the helpless subject for a test of her sensualism and her fearfulness.

At the end of the corridor the nursery door stood a little open, so that the night light left burning there fell in a band across the floor; and for as long as she stood thus motionless Milly saw only that light, and when at last she moved forward her eyes never left it. . . . Her steps were quick and cautious, she bent forward as she walked, and her mouth twitched and twisted with something she whispered—something about a bedroom door—a door doubtless closed now, but against which one might still nevertheless lay one's ear and listen—and listen. . . .

She reached the nursery threshold, waited a second, pushed the door tremblingly a little farther open, stepped in. . . .

Had this but been the Milly of last week—of yesterday—of a mere two hours ago—there would have been for her a reason to warn, and a logic—that queer, clear, consistent logic!—to foresee that she shouldn't be alone in that nursery—that on this of all occasions, in this of all hours, she must all but inevitably encounter those other presences whose right to be there immeasurably surpassed her own, whose purposes—for love, for dark tremendous evil—had a magnitude before which her little soul could but gape and quake:—Katherine, tall, handsome, imperious, with her back against that bedroom door, her arms outspread to bar passage through it, her cold unanswerable gaze bent straight into the face of Phoebe; and Phoebe, tall too, and black and evil and terrible, determined to pass that threshold, knowing that it must be tonight or perhaps never, moving back and forth before her enemy, waiting—advancing, retreating, trying first one side and then the other—for hours—hours—hours. . . . And the Milly of yesterday would have known—known with a conviction that was itself a horror—that to look—upon those two thus was not—was not, ever!—for her. . . .

. . . But this woman, as she pushed the nursery door a little farther open and stepped within—this woman was not the Milly of last week—nor of yesterday—nor yet, even, of a mere two hours ago.

*   *   *

. . . She seemed to be lying—lying deep, deep—in a sea of darkness—in an agony of cold, of pain . . . could hear, ever so faintly, the sound of moaning . . . knew the sound, dimly, as her own. . . . The burden of blackness seemed to lift, to be displaced from somewhere—somehow from within herself—by a kind of dawn. . . .

Her eyes opened . . . closed . . . opened—recognized the staircase—narrowed with her effort to remember—closed with her failure. . . .

Again the darkness, and pain, and cold; and then later, another, clearer return, which made no effort now to remember, but noted that it was morning—growing light. . . . Then they—the children—would be leaving! And here she—right in their path. . . . They mustn't find her—mustn't find her like this!

She got to her knees—to her feet—moved a little in the direction of her own room, keeping to the wall for support . . . but it wasn't light after all, was it? It was getting dark—black—

But the light dawned yet again, and she tried anew—and this time, though she failed of her room, she was safely out of sight when, far down the corridor, the nursery door opened and her children emerged. Richard's eyes were covered, and Mary's looked nowhere but at her husband.

Huddled in the shadow, Milly watched them approach, turn at the stairs, disappear. A cry rose in her throat to stop them—to keep them a little longer; but she choked it down—knowing that, at best, she could have kept them but a little—little while. . . .

Part 3
The Lady who served a child

It might seem that six years of discussion—of the kind of discussion, at any rate, that the twins were capable of giving it—would have left them at least some measure of agreement, some sameness of view, upon their subject—the subject, that is, of which Milly had left such a re-markable account for their consideration. But, under the urgent provo-cation of Mary's request, as they looked now for guidance to a decision among the results of their abundance of talk, they could but see that it had yielded not agreement—not, by any means, the clear certainty of opinion required for the safe right action they wished now to take—but merely a group of carefully developed half-fearful possibilities. Milly hadn't of course failed, in leaving them the subject, to leave them also her own lucid interpretation of everything about it; but the twins hadn't accepted that. Poor Milly's opinions had at best never seemed of much worth to them; and these late years—lonely, empty years which might have softened their judgments on many points—had made little differ-ence on this. Perhaps, though, this one denial had been purposely de-liberate: perhaps, until now, they hadn't *wanted* explanation and understanding, hadn't wanted their perplexities cleared, their questions answered—had, rather, preferred to keep them, to keep their whole vague shadowy substance, alive between them; for after all they could hardly have failed to see that if, by some fatal acceptable solution, they were to lose it, to spoil its mystery, there would be almost nothing left on earth for them to talk about.

An illness of Emma's had at all events, in the last three months, kept their minds on nearer things; so that now, in their bedroom where the gaunt old lady sat propped up in bed, and with Mary's letter on the coverlet between them, they had come back to their subject, and par-ticularly to their niece's part in it, with freshened vigour and a new view indeed of its importance. This time, though, it wasn't simply to talk; it was to arrive, as directly and definitely as they might, at a conclusion—first, as to how much Mary herself had known, what she had thought, about the peculiar, the vague and sinister, conditions of their house; and second as to what those conditions might hold of evil promise for Mary's five-year-old son! . . . So if they argued it was not, certainly, for argument's sake; if they did go over much old ground, did say things already said on a hundred other occasions, they did so swiftly, and reached, remarkably soon, a point at which Emma could pronounce, in words sufficiently familiar to them both, her theory—"Well, I suppose Mary simply doesn't know—or at least doesn't believe—as much as we do, or as Milly did."

And Lucia didn't, this time, disagree. Instead, after a silence and with a decisive head-shake, she conclusively did the opposite—"No, she doesn't! We've no single scrap of a reason to think otherwise; and it's unthinkable that if she even so much as suspected she'd want that child—that baby—to come here. . . ."

But if this seemed sufficiently to settle their long-nourished uncertainty with regard to Mary's awareness, it by no means solved their problem—answered not at all that other question of what, in their house, Mary's small son might be exposed to. And though they faced this now squarely enough, they were soon to find—and of course but naturally—that they could do little else, little better than merely to face it: it could not, simply, with its inscrutable depths, be looked into. . . . Abruptly then, determinedly, even boldly, at the end of several seconds of silence, Lucia gave up trying to look into it—took an attitude in which conjecture should have no place—and which, too, constituted a departure indeed from the willing mystification which, in these late quiet years, had dealt so gently with their subject—"After all, Sister, we must remember that we've had no real evidence of our own that there is—or ever was—anything for anybody to *be* afraid of."

"We've surely, though, enough of Milly's!"

"I know: Milly made a good deal of the danger . . . but Milly imagined things." Lucia paused a minute, then made, for her negative attitude, a small concession—"If there was anything to be afraid of it couldn't have amounted to much—could it?—or Mary herself wouldn't have escaped it. She lived here for ten years. If she was safe, why—?"

"But Milly didn't say—and didn't imagine either—that Mary was responsible for her own safety. . . . You know what Milly thought!"

"Yes—" Lucia's answer was prompt—"and if she was right—about Mary's being 'protected,' as she called it, in that unnatural way—doesn't it follow that Mary's child would be too—in the same way?"

They looked at each other over this for a considerable silence, until Emma, ignoring the question, a little accusingly asked—"You don't believe Mary *was* protected, do you?"

Lucia considered; then quietly confessed—"No—I don't think I do. I don't want to believe it. If the child is to come here, I'd much rather believe that no protection, of that kind, is necessary—will ever be necessary." And then, as in answer to the searching, waiting, unsatisfied look in Emma's face, she concluded—"Don't be surprised; we must be definite—frank. It's never been necessary before, and I've really not asked myself—not known—until now, what I thought about it all. . . . What do *you* think?"

Emma, lying back now, tired, upon her pillows, was far less sure: "Well, you know, Milly was convinced—I can't forget Milly's conviction. . . ."

I

For all the reference they made henceforth to its substance, this talk might have ended with a mutual determination never to discuss the topic again; for, as happened, no mention of the boy's safety, or of the two women in whose invisible hands it might or might not still incomprehensibly rest, was to be voiced by either sister until this day was already long in the past. It was, perhaps, a wise silence; for after all, in equal possession as they were of all the shadowy evidence, their difference of view would doubtless have been far less likely to diminish, under discussion, than to lead them into profitless disagreement. To have talked about it, simply, would have been futile if nothing worse.

They seemed to recognize this, even as they looked for a second or two into each other's eyes on the conclusion, with its divergent view, of this discussion; and, with an abruptness that neither could well have failed to note, their talk turned in another direction—the direction that led straight to their decision. They paused long enough by the way to observe that, in view of past persistent invitations, they had come confessedly a bit late in the day to a consideration of the child's safety in their house; but they soothed their consciences on this point by remembering that after all their wish to have him here had simply never figured him without his mother. They didn't, however, make much now of that; the exigency from which Mary had found it pressingly necessary to appeal to them left no alternative, if he were to come at all, to his coming alone—left, in fact, little time for consideration of any sort whatever. . . .

They took time nevertheless, in the afternoon, quite unreservedly to admit their hesitancy, and its reason, to their good old friend the doctor, and to ask his advice. Plainly pleased with the prospect of the child's coming, he made no single suggestion of an objection beyond one amused question as to what they thought they'd do with the boy when they got him; and after taking in without comment but with an attention surprised, deepening, incredulous, at some points strangely keen, their all but incredible doubts, he at last, with rather surprising brevity, gave them, for their decision, the last needed word of support— "It seems to me you have built a remarkably definite objection upon very questionable premises; and I'd advise you to think no more about it. If that youngster doesn't come here he'll have to be placed somewhere with strangers—for certainly Mary can't take him with her. And if you're thinking of dangers—well, I'm sure that the kind—the very certain ones—he'd be threatened with in some boarding school or what not deserve a good deal more consideration than whatever it is you're afraid of here. I should say by all means let him come!"

And so, when the doctor left them an hour later, he carried with him their answer to Mary's letter—the answer that was to bring them the little boy.

*　　*　　*

From then on, their attention was taken up practically to the exclusion of everything else with the abundance of things the prospect of his visit gave them to think about and to do. They discussed it over Emma's breakfast; the nursery was completely "done over"; the springs and mattress in the adjoining bedroom were unnecessarily renewed; Lucia had brought down from the attic and opened a box of Mary's father's toys; and their talk about it still went on when they should have been asleep. For of course it was a circumstance of the highest importance to them—an adventure, verily, which, in their empty old lives where the smallest of interests was serious, established itself at once as a case whose every contingency they must be at pains to anticipate. But it was not by any means of course altogether a case for pleasurable enthusiasm; there were hours in abundance when they made a great deal indeed of their responsibility. What, they asked each other blankly, did a child eat, for instance? What hours did it sleep? How did it play? Suppose it were to fall ill! . . . And what should be done about its clothes, its habits, its training? Would he require a nurse, or wasn't he old enough to take care of himself? . . . They knew nothing about babies— and especially, they quaintly acknowledged, about boy-babies.

It was a distinct comfort, on this point, to remind each other that they still had Martha Stroub—that *she* ought to know something about them surely, since she had had several. And indeed, from the hour they told her of the boy's coming until the time, months later, when she was carried away crippled and ill, Mrs. Stroub proved a veritable treasure to them. She took the news, on this first day, with a short large-eyed speechless stare; then for some joyous reason they didn't understand she cried a bit; and last she disposed like magic of all their fears and uncertainties—of everything they had found it but too easy to make a difficulty of. Later, when the child had come—when he stood for the first time inside their door—it was Mrs. Stroub who, despite her rheumatism and with Lucia standing awkwardly by, went down on one knee, took his two hands, and welcomed him. It was Mrs. Stroub too who, while the twins could only watch with admiration, established him in the house—managed with an ease that left them frankly wondering these awesome details of his care—of his diet, his dress, his rest and play, his laundry, the care of his teeth, the length of his very finger-nails. And then it was through Mrs. Stroub that they learned—or began to learn, for that was all it amounted to for some time—to know him—learned in full detail the items of his wardrobe, the titles of his books, the words of his prayers, the things he liked to eat, what he thought of their house and themselves, and a stock of tastes and concepts of such colour and variety as to make them ask each other in sheer astonishment where in the world he had got them.

Yet for all these details, for all their careful interest in him, he remained to a degree disappointingly hard for them to understand. They had hoped, had expected, to know him thoroughly and easily: they had known Mary well enough; and her son, supposedly, would be like her. But beyond a certain point—which, however, they couldn't just definitely fix—he wasn't; there were differences springing, doubtless, from his father whom they had never wholly understood either, or, perhaps, from the mere fact of his sex. He had, in perfect copy, his mother's round-eyed frankness, her smile, her clear good nature, her explicit speech; but he had too his father's hair, brown and fine like silk, and his father's slim straight body; and he showed them long pensive periods in which they could but wonder what he was thinking about, and a queer little knack of sensing the motives of the things they said to him, a manner of weighing his answers, of making them wait, while he smiled like an angel at their expectancy, for what he had to say—and these were not manners of Mary's. . . .

He slept, of course, in the nursery bedroom, played more or less reverently with his grandfather's toys, for one of which, an ancient German music box, he showed an especial fondness. He enjoyed the run of the house, except for two locked rooms—the one nobody had entered for half a century, and Phoebe's—and soon, except for these two, there was not a nook in the building unfamiliar to him. The servants—mostly friends of magnificent Katherine and charming Mary—treated him as befitted a little prince; and by way of response he preferred, next to Mrs. Stroub, the cook. Of the twins, Emma was from the outset his favourite—because, reported Mrs. Stroub, he felt sorry for anybody sick.

II

It was perhaps inevitable that before a very great while the twins came seriously to face what they more or less rightly called the problem of his entertainment. In time—enough time to have exhausted the house and its quiet schedule of newness and interest for the child, to have permitted the complete absorption of his habits, his requirements, his whole small life, by the unswerving routine about him—it had grown clear to them that in the combination of the boy with his environment something was wrong. They had first wondered about it and then worried about it—had talked it over at length, and at last, failing to understand it, unable otherwise to explain it, had begun gravely to wonder if something were not the matter with the boy.

Of this possibility—of the whole disturbing subject—they of course found, from day to day, a great deal to say to each other; and as his stay lengthened, and while concern and conjecture were leading them nowhere, their sense of the substance of their problem continued to find but too sufficient range of evidence to look to for support—evidence of their own eyes which saw plainly the child's activity slacken, his capacity for interest steadily drop, his characteristic vividness pale, his contentment lessen; and evidence in detail of Mrs. Stroub's of the manner of his single-handed play—of listless hours in the nursery with his toys, his drawing pad, his picture books—of his journeyings, sometimes aimless sometimes not, in and about the house—of strange games he invented and in which she tried heroically to participate—of hours spent in the grounds with a pile of pebbles, or flat on his back watching the sky—of the way in which he would drop his play to listen for minutes together to the voices of children from beyond the wall of the grounds, or would press his face against the gate to watch them passing in the street. . . .

They of course did, in their unskilled way, what they could—with proper stories, with talk, with dignified gifts from down town, with good things from the kitchen—but for all his charming little gratitude they saw no real success for their efforts. They asked Mrs. Stroub for suggestions; but the best she could do for them was to admit that in the twelve or fourteen waking hours of his day it wasn't much to be wondered at that he found time often heavy on his hands; and the good lady a little lamely pointed out, in extenuation of her lack of anything better to offer, that an experience in raising several children in a small house didn't of necessity equip one to raise a single child in a great house. . . . They turned then, in a frank bid for the benefit of another experience and a fuller knowledge, to the doctor.

And the doctor responded like a man who had felt the question in the wind—had known long ago how he would answer it—"He needs other children, of course! He's lonesome—lonesome! Call in your neighbors' youngsters; get him playmates; give him a party!" And if this reply—for its quick simplicity and its unheard-of prescription—left them staring a little, the doctor let them stare. Plainly, he had meant what he said; and indeed it would hardly have been remarkable if he had said a good deal more—had told them plainly that the mysterious something which concerned them as being "the matter" with the child was nothing in the world but that his delicate little emotional machinery was going numb under the pressure of the atmosphere in which he lived—that the air of their house, cold with order, thick with old interests and old practices, dark with incomprehensible shadows, rested too, too heavily upon him. Of course they didn't—couldn't—know it; and the doctor, perhaps because he knew them so well, let pass the opportunity to tell them; but there indeed it lay, that atmosphere, upon the child, upon them, upon everything, evenly, envelopingly, like a darkness—or perhaps, for a little boy, like some grey disquieting dream, where one might wander wonderingly and troubled in the stillness, but where play, and fun, and laughter had no place.

The twins accepted, at all events, their friend's suggestion, and gave the child his party. The councils they held about it, the task they made of acquainting themselves with how it should properly be done, the preparations they made, the excitement they suffered, were worthy indeed of a great occasion; and if it cost them something in peace of mind and sent poor Emma back to bed for two days, they faced each other when it was over with tired, gladdened faces and outdid themselves in assurances that Dicky's pleasure would have compensated for fifty times their trouble. . . .

But the children, most of whom had come with slow feet and awed faces into this house at which they had peeked through the gates and about which strange stories were told—the children, as time resumed again in the house its grey unvaried march, never returned. And then the poor twins, talking it over with injured expressions, couldn't understand, and finally spoke of it no more. And weeks went by and Dicky, who had talked at first incessantly of his party, mentioned it less and less frequently; Emma was up and about again; Mrs. Stroub, with joints stiffening in the waning summer, predicted a wet fall; and the doctor came and went, drank tea and talked, patted the boy kindly upon the head—and (to mitigate, perhaps, the failure of his prescription) brought him, one day in October, a puppy.

But then, even while this acquisition of a new companion was still recent, it was but too completely offset, for Dicky, by the loss of an old one: Mrs. Stroub's rheumatism, developing lately with a malice, began to deprive him of days of her comradeship, and finally, because the care it made necessary could not be given at the house, took her away altogether.

*   *   *

On that day, which was to mark for him the beginnings of more changes than one, with eyes large with interest he watched his good friend go—followed the stretcher to the door, beyond which, because of the rain, he might not pass—raced upstairs to his window whence he could see the procession to the ambulance—watched them place her in it, close its doors, drive it, on great cushioned wheels, away. For many minutes then—because there was nothing else to do—he stayed at the window, his face against the cool glass, gazing into the deserted grounds and street—until, at the sound of her footfall, he turned to face Emma.

The good old lady still wore the marks of her illness. She looked tired—weary; her shoulders drooped; the grey dress hung loose upon her body; and in her white sunken face the large pale eyes were in a rather startling way more prominent than ever. But her unloveliness meant nothing to Dicky; he seemed not to see it—seemed instead, when he had crossed the room to the chair she had taken, and her bony hands had closed over his, to look past her helpless ugliness into something else—some intention—which lay as yet within her mind. . . .

"When," he quietly asked, "will she come back?"

"As soon, my dear, as she's better. We hope that won't be long."

He was silent for a minute. Then—"I wish she wasn't sick."

"We all wish that; but we all get sick sometimes—and get well again too. Now, you see, Mrs. Stroub has gone away because she's sick, but here am I, getting well again, to take her place. So it's all right after all—isn't it?"

He wasn't so sure—less sure, at all events, than honest—"But you're not Mrs. Stroub, anyway."

Emma's answer was almost humble—"I know, but you'll find me a very willing substitute. If I can't make up stories, I can always read them. I can work puzzles too, and play games—if they're gentle games.

And when I was young—fifty years ago—I could draw pictures. Perhaps I could learn again—perhaps even teach a little boy . . ."

And thus, in surely the quaintest bid for his favour that Dicky was ever to hear, the frail old lady offered herself, her confidence, her meagre talents, to him; and whatever its promise meant to him, she couldn't fail to see that he found in its expression something deeply, gratefully welcome—something which, when their talk was ended, had at least left them better friends.

*   *   *

And so, reduced to the association of two ancient ladies and his puppy, and kept by the cold and wet of the autumn far too much indoors, Dicky made now what he could of an existence colourless, lifeless, changeless, which, like a darkness, had settled inescapably upon him. Bravely indeed Emma actualized her promises—drew the promised pictures—listened and talked to him about anything he chose to discuss—read his stories and verses until she fairly knew them by heart. . . . It was his habit to appear before her at least once each day, to hand her, already open, his favourite book, and to seat himself at her side for their invariable beginning—

> "'When at home alone I sit
> And am very tired of it,
> I have just to close my eyes
> To go sailing through the skies—
> To go sailing far away
> To the pleasant land of play . . .'"

But the charm of Stevenson, supplemented often enough by that of other authors and by their own gentle talk, usually paled toward the end of an hour and left them both tired at last. Then, with grave thanks, he would take his book and go away, and in a few minutes, down the long corridor from the nursery would come the sad thin tinkle of his grandfather's music box.

All his habits were fixed, all his practices regular. They allowed him, less and less inclined to mischief as he seemed to become, to do very much as he liked when he was alone; but there wasn't, truly, very much to do. They supposed, and rightly enough, that when he was out of their sight, he was gone, with his puppy at his heels, exploring in the great old house; they would come upon him standing before some picture, lost in frowning contemplation; they found him not seldom looking hard at the blank faces of the two doors that were closed to him;

and they frequently caught him studying their own faces, as though he might be expecting or hoping for something to appear which was not now there. . . .

III

Autumn deepened into winter: the rains gave place to snows—the snows that were to lie until spring; and there came periods of severe and protracted cold. And meanwhile the concern of the twins on the question of the boy's amusement, of the whole general case of his reaction to his surroundings, had reached its peak, had persisted there disquietingly indeed for a time, had begun at last to drop, and had, by midwinter, quite dwindled away. Whatever had given rise to it in the first place was apparent to them no more. The boy had altered and so had they. They were all again content.

The change in Dicky was, however, a difference notably more positive than the mere easy extinction of anxiety which constituted their own; in Dicky's case, indeed, as it had become by degrees clearer and clearer, there had shown nothing negative at all. What had been mere lifeless passivity in him had plainly been supplanted by something else—a reawakened interest—a cheerfulness almost, which twinkled at them from eyes that had been too long dull, from flushed cheeks too long pale, from quick vivacious speech too long rare and serious. There were other symptoms too—definite physical differences in his behaviour, which had come into evidence too gradually for the sisters now to fix their beginning, but which were there not in the least to be denied. Conspicuous among these, besides his appetite, was the noise he made—noises of his and his puppy's scamperings through the upper corridors, of rolling balls and tumbling blocks, of callings and of barks. Also, his entreaties to be allowed outside had all but ceased. And even the manner of his intercourse with the sisters had altered. He spent noticeably less time with them, for one thing, and, for another, he had changed their conversation from a habit too dull for his taste to one rather too lively for their own. The difficulty here was to keep up with him—to follow the shifts of his thinking, to guide his understanding, to meet his lucid erratic little logic, and, above all, to answer his questions—questions born, seemingly, with every breath he drew, and about everything—about themselves, their house, the doctor, the servants, his puppy, dogs in general, children, fairies, angels. . . .

If they frequently failed to answer him, it was not always, of course, because they couldn't; not seldom it was because they were unable to make certain of what he wanted to know. Such an instance was one which arose, once, with a subject suggested by his book: Emma was reading, and with the first two lines—

>*"When children are playing alone on the green*
>*In comes the playmate that never was seen . . ."*

—Dicky stood up, his attention suddenly sharpened, watching her— waiting for her to stop. She let him wait—finished the poem—before pausing to hear what he had to say—for clearly he had something. He returned, first, to the verse itself, repeating after her own manner—

>*"Nobody heard him and nobody saw,*
>*His was a picture you never could draw"*—

and then, abruptly—"but it wasn't a *man* was it? Does it have to be a man?"

Emma hesitated. "Well—no; not a man that you could really see— not one that walks and talks—"

"But I mean couldn't it be a lady?"

She looked at him blankly, and if it came into her mind to ask him what he was driving at, she patiently didn't—"A lady? . . . But why a lady?—what sort of lady?"

"Well—" he paused, a little perplexed now himself; and his words, when they came, did almost as little for her question as hers had done for his. "Well, just a lady—kind of tall-like—instead of a man."

To satisfy him then she agreed to suppose that a lady might do as well; and the subject changed, forgotten in a moment by him, recog- nized by the sisters as merely another little mystery of his imagination.

With his improvement—or perhaps more definitely with the grow- ing abundance of these mental sproutings for which they were so often at a loss to account—there developed also a fairly distinct divergence of interest in him on the part of the sisters. Lucia, seldom with him nowa- days, seemed to have passed the point at which her concern with what he thought and said and did could increase; and she frankly admitted that he had got so far beyond her reach that she felt helpless of ever grasping him completely now at all. But Emma, disappointed if he ne- glected her, eager to satisfy his wishes, faithful to her promises of the day of Mrs. Stroub's removal, continued bravely, fondly, to make his in- terests her own—watched him, talked with him, spent a good part of every day in his company, followed the trains of his thought as far as his words and her imagination could carry her. . . . Strangely enough, this difference of attitude on the part of the twins—this first instance for near half a century in which they had behaved as different persons, in which their thoughts and words and acts had not been as one—seemed to disturb them very little: the boy was happy, and if this shift of intimacies which had isolated Lucia and attached Emma to him could keep him happy, Lucia could evidently dispense, in silence if nothing else, with Emma—though she did once remark that the new companionship, taking character as it had only after the development of his unaccountable little independence of any companionship whatever, appeared to have ripened rather late.

But there, at all events, the companionship was, and whatever it meant to Lucia or to Dicky, it came to mean a great deal to Emma—for interest, for amusement, for tenderness; and it led at last to a discovery.

This took place, or began to take place, on one of their afternoons in the nursery where, occupied with crochet hook and carpet-warp, she had spoken no word for half an hour, while he, with houses and fences, trees and animals and men, had built a tiny city upon the floor—talking steadily meanwhile to an imagined playmate—a constant one, too, apparently, for she had heard its name before—

". . . and here comes the man on the horse—riding, riding, and— Beeba! why did you put that house there? That's the street; and the man can't get by! . . . There, now he can. . . . Here he is; now Beeba, you feed his horse."

Emma paused to listen, watched him awhile, resumed her work, stopped again, and spoke—"Dicky, come here a moment."

Surprised—it was evident he had forgotten her—he turned; then got up and stood before her. She let him wait a few seconds—eighteen stitches finished this row—and then "Who," she asked, "is Beeba?"

He smiled—the faintest trace of a smile and almost wholly in his eyes—"Well, she's a girl I play with."

Emma waited again. It wasn't just easy to pick the right question, and she rejected several before going on—"You've been talking to her here for quite awhile, but whenever I've looked up to see her she's been gone. . . . My eyes must be getting bad." She looked at him now, seriously—"Is she here now—right now?"

His small smile persisted—"Oh yes—she's been here all the time. Didn't you see how she put that house right in the middle of the road so nobody could get past?"

"No," answered Emma, "I didn't see that; I only heard you scolding her for it. . . . Tell me—what does Beeba look like?"

Before her gravity his smile had faded; yet she couldn't have told, as he looked now steadily away from her towards his little city, whether he was describing some object or merely inventing his answer. "Well," he at any rate at last said, "her dress is white—white, but kind of blue."

As he paused here she pressed him, ever so gently—"And what color eyes has she?"

Watching him now she saw his look—always steadily away from her—narrow a little, as though he were indeed trying to discern, in his corner, the thing she had asked; and then suddenly, with his attention still fixed, he smiled—a quick amused smile that was like a response—for all the world as if he had seen, across the room, a small pair of eyes suddenly opened grotesquely wide to aid him. "I guess," he answered, "they're blue too."

"You guess. . . . Well—are they like mine?"

He shook his head—"No. And they're not really truly blue either. But I mean they ought to be—they *would* be blue—don't you see?"

Doubtless she didn't see—not as clearly, in any event, as he seemed to; but it was hardly a detail worth insisting upon, and she tried, a little at random, for another—"But you haven't told me yet just who she is; I don't seem to know her at all. Where does she live?"

"Here," he promptly answered—"right here—upstairs." But then—for she looked dubious, and her eyes demanded the best accuracy he could give—he retracted—"But I don't know where she lives really—when she's not here . . ." He paused for a second's thought, and then concluded, ". . . Maybe not anywhere."

For this, which seemed even to surprise Dicky himself a little, Emma had a blank look indeed; and her next speech, in the manner of its utterance hardly less than in its conspicuous difference of subject, seemed consciously, deliberately, to set the question of Beeba's residence for the moment aside—"Shouldn't you like, sometime, to have her lunch with us?"

"Beeba?"

She nodded. And now for ten seconds her eyes searched his face not a whit more deeply than his searched her own—searched it wondering undisguisedly what she meant by this, and concealing not at all a resentful little suspicion that she might be laughing at him. But Emma's face, as serious, as earnest as his own, was surely a plain reassurance against his doubts; and in a minute he had brightened again, taken up her suggestion, fortified it with one of his own—and the engagement was settled for tomorrow.

IV

Accordingly next day a service was placed for the guest, and promptly on time Dicky, in pongee and velvet and patent leather, appeared in the dining room doorway. He paused there a moment to look, much as he had looked suspiciously at Emma yesterday, at each of the three old faces turned towards him—at Emma's first, then at Lucia's, and last and longest at the doctor's; but no shade of a laugh was there to be seen, and, after a moment, with a smile which more than anything else a little loftily approved their gravity, he turned, extended his hand as to someone still standing in the shadow behind him, and said, "Come on, Beeba; they're waiting."

Whatever they thought, at the table, they concealed; no eye was turned from him and no word spoken as he advanced, with dignity and still as though he were not alone, towards the table; and only when they were seated and Dicky's head was bowed for grace did the eyes of the sisters meet. It was to be the last look they would risk until the meal was over, and they took it, full and silent and gravely wondering, while they could.

Evidently they had arranged to dispense with the servant, for soup was ready served upon the table, salad and pudding had been placed, plates and tea stood at Emma's elbow, and a vegetable dish and casserole lay hot before her on the table. As they took up their spoons Emma, noting a frown on the boy's face, asked, "What's the matter, Dicky?"

"I think," he returned, "that Beeba ought to have a cushion or something to sit on. She's as little as me."

Eyeing him across the empty chair between them, she after a moment quietly answered, "You may get her a cushion if you like." And when it was placed and he had taken his chair again, he looked first pleasedly at the elevation his small companion's face should have occupied, then up at Emma, and then, satisfied, back at his plate. As they ate then for some minutes without speaking, he seemed of them all quite the most at ease; and if he felt the doctor's look upon him, or was aware of Lucia's perplexed frown, he gave no sign to show it. Once he remarked, towards Beeba, that this was his favorite soup, and asked how she liked it. And last, when the plates were set aside—all empty but that one—he assured Emma that Beeba had enjoyed that soup.

It was in the air, however, that for all his little ease he as yet wholly trusted none of them—none, at least, but Emma—not to laugh at him. But a little later the doctor, beginning a conversation with the twins about something in which the child had no interest, must have reassured him, for in their first silence Dicky spoke straight at him—"I just told Beeba she better eat her carrots or she won't grow. And that's right, isn't it?"

The doctor, serious as the boy himself, kept him waiting not an instant—"Indeed it is! We must eat carrots if we want to grow!"

The child looked heavily into the untouched dish beside Beeba's plate—"Now see, Beeba? You heard what he said—and he's a doctor!" But in the next second, with a changed expression and an inconsequence which left his moral nowhere, he remarked, "But it doesn't matter, I guess; Beeba won't grow any more anyhow."

From his own expression then the doctor must have been within a breath of uttering the "Why not?" so obviously the rejoinder to this; but Emma, with the slightest of headshakes, caught his eye, and he said nothing. Lucia, however, overriding their delicacy, turned to the boy—"Why not, Dicky? Why won't she grow any more?"

He met it, after a moment, with a finality that she could hardly not respect—"Well, you know, she's not *like* us." And before the wordless remonstrance of her two older companions, Lucia, satisfied or not, didn't press him further; and nothing more was said until, when the course was finished, he explained to Emma the fullness of Beeba's dish—"It's too bad about her carrots, Aunty; but she really doesn't care for carrots."

Emma's response was easy and prompt and kind—"Well, my dear, we didn't know. Now you must find out what she likes, and next time she comes we'll ask cook to be sure and have some for her."

She caught, on this, a pleased encouraging look from the doctor; but she saw too in her sister's face a deepening disapproval. Lucia watched the boy a bit more narrowly now than seemed needful, too, while his pudding disappeared, and her next question, spoken after Emma had excused him and Beeba from the table, had about it less of the indulgent gentleness of her sister's words than anything yet said to him—"Dicky—did you tell your Aunt Emma that Beeba lives upstairs?"

She had brought him around before her and, holding both his hands, was looking straight into his eyes. Her seriousness—the evidence of its intention—clearly embarrassed him a little, and he glanced towards Emma before answering. His reply then was simply—"Yes, Aunty;" but Emma added as a reminder, "Remember, Lucia, he qualified that."

"You see, Dicky," Lucia went on, "Aunt Emma and I knew nothing about her being there. Could you tell us—tell us—where she came from?"

Dicky thought a moment, and shook his head—"They don't come from *places*. They're just there, when I want them."

"*They?* Are there others—more besides this one?"

"Lucia—" remonstrated Emma—"gently, gently! Dicky dear, how many others are there?"

The boy, his hands still held in Lucia's, answered Emma across the table—"Well—as many as I want, I guess."

"And it's ever so fortunate, isn't it, to have as many playmates as one wants. But you're neglecting Beeba; isn't she waiting for you?"

The promptness of this rejoinder, which had come quick and quiet while Lucia and the doctor looked at each other over the child's last words, gave it all the look of an effort to free him for the moment from further questioning; and Emma's unconcealed relief as he disappeared through the door amply confirmed that appearance. But her successful little stroke was evidently neither understood nor approved by Lucia, whose puzzled displeased look she had now to face—"I don't understand why you did that, Sister. I wanted to question him. He ought to be questioned."

Emma's reason was clear enough to herself—"I don't think, though, that you were doing it in the right way. Your eagerness frightened him. It would be a mistake to destroy his confidence—"

But Lucia had little patience for that—"I think it a greater mistake not to put a stop, immediately, to this unnatural business of these playmates. The very idea of a five-year-old child inventing such a—a falsehood! There's no telling what it might lead to. Do you think he should be encouraged in it, for pity's sake? I thought children should be taught to tell the truth!"

She had turned now indignantly to face the doctor, and he, with half a smile for her vehemence, answered for Emma—"You take it, my dear, far too seriously. It's neither so dangerous nor so unusual as you seem to think. Children—and especially lonely ones—have had make-believe playmates ever since they've had imaginations. If you think Dicky's case so extraordinary, what do you think of a little boy I know who has an entire family—mother, father, and three children, all named—living in the palm of his hand; or of another who spends his play-time almost nowhere but in one corner of his father's apple-orchard, because that corner is inhabited; or of a four-year-old daughter of a friend of mine who couldn't be happy until her parents had put an extra bed in her room for a companion that comes every night to sing her to sleep?"

The old gentleman talked easily, seemed to like it; and as their eyes remained upon him and neither spoke, he went on—"'Falsehoods' isn't the name for these things. We have no way of judging the vividness with which youngsters see them; and after all, aren't they as legitimate as—well, two-thirds of the things we tell them and read to them?

"As for Dicky, with his remarkable little imagination, I should say simply that the inevitable has happened. I remember he was pathetically lonely here a few months ago—and we talked about it, and tried, and failed, to do anything for him. He wanted—needed—playmates; so he made them. I wouldn't interfere if I were you. Let him enjoy them. They won't hurt him; they help make him happy; and, anyhow, you couldn't take them away from him now if you tried. And if you're determined to try in spite of me—and of your sister—let me advise you to go ever so gently. It doesn't—it can't—appear to him as unnatural as it does to you, for he isn't in the least concerned with merely understanding it, and if you don't approach him—approach his case—in some way through his own way of looking at it, you'll simply confuse him and come out nowhere."

Lucia hadn't taken her eyes off him, but her face, changing slowly while he talked, wore now as he stopped a look not so much of conviction as of injury. She had begun, beyond doubt, by being sufficiently sure of her ground, had acted—or at least had spoken—with as good an intent toward the boy as either of these other two; and to have had her effort blocked as her sister had blocked it, to have had the ground taken from beneath her feet as the doctor, their nearest friend, had fairly taken it—to have been treated, in short, more like a child than Dicky himself—was hardly of course the kind of treatment to leave a wilful old lady wholly unresentful. She didn't answer him.

There was, however, little time for her silence to be noticed, for Emma, looking, oddly enough, yet less convinced than Lucia, had a question for the doctor—"What do you think *is* his way of looking at it?"

He shook his head—"I wish I knew! I only know that it must be immeasurably different from ours. Remember, he can believe in fairies quite as easily as he can in doctors, as easily that a bird could turn into an egg as that an egg can become a bird. The difference between us, in imagination, in credulity, in points of view, is pretty much, I should suppose, the difference of our measures of experience—of our lengths of life. And we've lived seventy years longer than he! We don't," he wound up, "know how he looks at things."

"You think, though," Emma pressed him, "that these companions of his are merely imagined—that he has to think about Beeba's dress before he can tell me the colour of it—that he has to invent her actions before he can laugh at them—"

Something in Lucia's face—her frown, the sharp intentness of her look—made Emma pause; but the doctor, looking a little as though he had heard a question whose point he didn't catch, answered, "I shouldn't say 'merely' imagined. I think that at that age they imagine with such vividness—"

"Well, I must say," Lucia broke in, "that this nonsense is beyond me! What in the world do you mean, Emma, by such a question? If the prodigious thing the doctor would have us believe the five-year-old imagination to be isn't enough to account for these—these inventions, how else *do* you propose to account for them?"

Emma, facing a little offendedly for the moment this outburst, turned towards the doctor, who, too, but with a different curiosity, awaited her answer—"I don't propose to account for them at all. . . . But," she added after a moment, "we mustn't quarrel about it."

Their friend, surprised, embarrassed—for the tension between his hostesses couldn't now be ignored—looked from one offended face to the other, and "No," he said, "it would never do to quarrel about it." And he turned the talk on something else. Perhaps he did so reluctantly, perhaps secretly wished that Lucia would, in spite of everything, insist at once on some better settlement for their subject; for he could hardly have failed to understand, as it stood, that his explanation—which, for all its apparent adequacy, had manifestly struck Lucia as extravagant and Emma as insufficient—had settled nothing whatever except that his view was different from theirs and that theirs were different from each other. Whatever he wished, however, whatever he wondered, he kept to himself, and did instead what he could in the next half hour—with light speech and with gossip which yesterday might well have interested them—in the more important matter of restoring peace between the sisters.

But they knew as little of reconciliations as they did of quarrels, and when he left them he could hardly not have seen that he left too their difference—their first genuine difference, perhaps, for forty years—still large between them. When the door had closed at his back, their eyes met for a short hard moment, and they separated with no word—Lucia to go to their bedroom, Emma to search out Dicky.

V

Entering the nursery she found him, an admiral's hat on his head, a toy sword of his grandfather's in his hand, and half turned towards her—as though, hearing her step, he had stopped some action to face the door.

He smiled her a welcome—"You walk just like Aunt Lucia—" and keeping his eyes on her while she didn't answer, he added—"You look like her too, now that you're better—a lot like her . . ."

The way he left this hanging too clearly invited a reply for her not to give it; but her words, as she crossed the room to a chair, bespoke no interest—sounded as though she might temporarily have put something else aside to say them—"Well, my dear, we are twins."

He seemed however unready, for some reason, to let the subject go—"That means you were born at the same time, doesn't it? Do people always look like each other when they're born at the same time?"

"Yes, I think so—especially," she went on, more directly, "if they live like Aunt Lucia and me. For you see, we've always *been* alike too—always lived in the same house, always done the same things, had the same kind of food to eat, the same books to read, the same people to talk to—until really we're almost like one person, instead of two."

He considered; "It's funny."

"Why?" she smiled.

"Well—" He hesitated; the thought, apparently, was too big for him—"It's funny there should be two of you, I mean. It'd be just the same if there was only one, if you're just the *same*—wouldn't it?"

She looked at him a moment without answering, but her astonishment concealed neither a flash of amusement nor her lapse, the next second, into a seriousness quite equal to his own—"I see. You mean that one of us must be unnecessary. But, you know, we're very important to each other, even if we're not to anybody else. It would seem very strange to us not to have each other—to talk to, to think of, to care for. We shouldn't be at all happy. I'm afraid," she concluded, "that we really couldn't do without each other."

He had stood, for this, directly in front of her, his feet far apart, his sword held behind him, his cockaded hat on the back of his head; and now, with the effect of her earnestness still upon him, he moved off towards his toy-cupboard, placed his hat in it and, half over his shoulder and across the breadth of the room, asked, "And don't you ever get mad?"

"At each other? Gracious no!"

He faced her now, with another question in his eyes, but before it sounded he visibly weighed it—in doubt perhaps as to whether he ought to ask it—"Wasn't she mad at you today at the table?"

"No, I think not."

"She *looked* mad."

Emma smiled. "I'm afraid you exaggerate. Come here." And when he had crossed the room to stand before her again, to take in at closer range the earnestness of her look, she went on, "Your Aunt Lucia and I could never really be angry with each other. That would make us both very unhappy—would be almost the worst thing that could happen to us. We simply would never permit it to happen, not for anything. . . . And I think what you took for anger today was really a little disappointment, because she hadn't known—because you hadn't told her more about Beeba."

"She doesn't like Beeba, does she?"

"Well, I'm afraid she doesn't know her."

"She didn't look at her today; I guess she didn't even see her."

Emma's eyes, fixed always on his, narrowed a bit; but though she seemed for the moment on the point of making some straighter speech she at last merely agreed—"Probably not."

His own look was steady too, and now, with the faintest trace of slyness, he smiled, "The doctor didn't see her either, did he? . . . Did you?"

She slowly shook her head, and, very gravely, echoed his question—"Did you?"

The manner of his answer was the manner of any gentleman's who expects to be believed—"I see them all, Aunty."

Emma held his eyes for a second more and then, rising, crossed to a window. Here, with her back to him and with a gentleness that concealed a far deeper interest than it exposed, she asked, "Why is it you haven't told us about them before?"

He didn't answer at once, and when she turned she could see a little wrinkle of perplexity in his forehead—much as though he were wondering why himself—"Well," he at last brought out, "you never asked me—and I don't think about them much except when they're with me—and you didn't know about them, and I guess I thought I *couldn't* tell you, really . . ."

She helped him out—"You mean you were afraid we wouldn't understand—is that it?"

"Yes. And," he added in a moment, "if you didn't understand you might think I was telling a fib."

She resumed her chair—"Well—we want to understand—as much as we can. Tell me something about them now—what they look like—what they do—where they come from . . . How," she specified, picking a point of easy departure for him, "how did they come the first time?"

"They didn't—not all at once," he promptly stated. "Only two; and the White Lady brought them."

"'The White Lady'?" Her quickness made him frown, but with the best smile she could produce and a prompt calmness she corrected that—"Is there a lady too?"

"Oh yes; three of them."

"Three?" She was careful now indeed. "The White Lady and who else?"

"The White Lady, and the Little Lady, and the Dark Lady. But the White Lady's the one!—the one that counts. She came first of all."

If other questions—and surely there were others in abundance now—crowded into her mind, Emma held them back. There were but too many to choose from anyway: she felt that almost helplessly—recognized, even in the confused rush of her own conjecture, the impossibility of drawing from him at once the fullness of detail she saw but too well the promise of. But she saw too that this was no opportunity to lose—that she must begin with him somewhere *now*, ask him something, draw him out somehow. Well, his tone in speaking of his White Lady had shown well enough that he might most easily have more to say of her; and so, before his look of curiosity for her blankness had had more than a minute to deepen, she brought him back to that—to his own last words—"You say she came first of all? Then maybe it would be best to tell me about her first of all. What does she look like?"

"Well, she's a tall lady—as tall as you; but she doesn't look like you. She looks—she looks—well, she looks like the Queen in the story book."

"'Very proud and very straight—'"

"Yes—and 'very good and kind.' She wants people to be happy. She makes me happy."

"Oh. . . . How?" Emma's quiet was intense.

"She comes to see me when I'm alone; she brought Beeba and all the children; she helps us play; she makes the Dark Lady stay away from me; and, you know, like it says in the book—

> "'*Tis she, when at night you go off to your bed,*
> *Bids you go to your sleep and not trouble your head;*
> *For wherever they're lying, in cupboard or shelf,*
> *'Tis she will take care of your playthings herself!'*"

"I see; and how long has she been—when did she first come? How long ago?"

It wasn't, apparently, very recently, for he frowned through several seconds of effort to remember—"It was after Mrs. Stroub went away, and—let's see—after the snow—Oh, I know! Remember when it snowed so deep and I couldn't go out, and you were sick and Aunt Lucia was busy and I got lonesome and wasn't very good? Well, that's when. That night I couldn't go to sleep, and I got up and looked out the window at the snow. I didn't feel very happy, either. Everything was so still and white, and the snow was coming down and coming down and coming down and I felt funny—like—like I wanted to cry. . . . And then I looked around and saw the White Lady."

He stopped, pleased, apparently, with his little narration, for he expectantly waited for her comment. But Emma had no praise for him— "But what else? Weren't you frightened? What was she doing? What did you do?"

He was frankly surprised—"I wasn't frightened: she was only smiling at me! . . . After a little while she came over by the window and looked at the snow with me; and I was glad she was there, and I didn't want to cry any more. Whenever I looked at her she just smiled, and it made me feel good." He looked at her again, but she only briefly encouraged him—

"Yes, and what then?"

"Well, after we'd watched the snow for a long time and I got sleepy, she went over and stood by my bed and I knew she wanted me to get in it; so I did. Then I went to sleep."

He paused here again, but without the least sign of unwillingness to continue, and she urged him on—"And what about the other two ladies, and the children?"

"Well, the White Lady used to come alone at first, but one day when I was playing that hiding game with Nippy, and he wouldn't hide and I got mad at him, she brought two children to help me play. After that more came—" he stopped for a short laugh—"sometimes there's lots of them. When we play soldier there are, and we march—I'm the captain, so I lead—we march up to the attic and around the boxes. . . ." He paused again, smiling; the picture was evidently as pleasing as it was vivid.

"They must be very quiet," suggested Emma; "we never hear them."

"Oh," he easily explained, a little as if he thought it shouldn't have been necessary, "they don't make *noise.*"

"But don't they laugh—don't they talk?"

He shook his head. "I'm the only one that talks—out loud. You see they—they don't have to."

"Don't have to?"

He explained again—"When they want something—when they want me to know something—well, I just know it."

If this was a little too much for her, Emma didn't press him for greater clearness. "Well," she said after a second's silence, "we'll talk about it again some other time. But you haven't told me about the other ladies—the dark one and the little one."

His face changed with an obvious drop of interest, and his reply was brief—"They don't do anything but just be there and watch."

"Watch?—Watch you?"

"The Dark Lady watches me, and the Little Lady watches her. I think she's afraid of her. . . . I don't think I like that Dark Lady very well."

"And what," quietly asked Emma, "do *they* look like?"

He frowned a little, as with an effort to recall some detail—"I don't know, only the Dark Lady's big and dark—like black—and the Little Lady's—well, just little. She always stands up or moves around, and the dark one sits down and wiggles her hands like she was doing something with them."

"Doing something. . . . Knitting perhaps."

He thought. "Yes—I guess that's what she's trying to do. Only, you know, she doesn't have any needles."

VI

Whatever impression this interview and some which followed it left with her, Emma didn't for several days attempt to talk about it with Lucia. It promised as yet but too certainly to be of no use—seemed altogether better, for the sake of any profit at all likely to be derived from discussion, to wait until Lucia should be a little more reasonably open to approach—until her aloofness, this offended, forbiddingly detached manner she had worn since Beeba's luncheon, and which made a difficulty of even the simplest intercourse with her, should have moderated somewhat. How soon that was likely to be Emma couldn't of course tell; but it brightened the prospect little indeed when, at the end of a week, the doctor visited them again and tentatively inquired after Dicky's playmates, for Lucia to answer—sharply, and before Emma could speak—to the explicit effect that she knew nothing about them, nor cared to. Nevertheless, however, as the natural issue of her view of the importance of what she knew, Emma did at last make an effort. It failed—as the doctor's inquiry had failed: Lucia, barely permitting her to begin, cut her short, and then in patient silence Emma heard the entire business, including herself, denounced as foolish if not downright sinful. Lucia would talk about it, she said, only to the end of having it stopped; otherwise she wouldn't hear a single word! and if Emma didn't soon come to her senses she, Lucia, should certainly write to Mary to have the child taken away, placed under stricter care, for his own good!

But Emma, quite as firm on her ground as Lucia on hers, wasn't just now to be silenced by a scolding—"You are mistaken about him—mistaken and unfair. . . . Yet I can't believe that you're satisfied to explain everything—the change in him, from his condition of a few months ago—in this way. You must see that it isn't—isn't *enough!*—"

Lucia rose to go, but Emma, rising too, held her a minute longer—"It would be shamefully unjust, you know, to send him away for—for the reason you have in mind; we simply mustn't think of it. But there is something else—possibly a really valid reason—which I—"

"The child isn't ill?"

"No—"

"If he's well—and certainly he's happy enough, I'll grant that—*I* can't believe there is any valid reason but my own for doing anything with him at all."

Emma's answer to this didn't come until her sister had passed through the door; and even then it had less the character of a reply than of an undirected thought, unwittingly spoken—"Well, he is happy. . . . Perhaps it's all right."

It must have been on her faith in that possibility then that she acted—or rather didn't again attempt to act—for some time afterward; for she made no further advance to Lucia, and days passed and they rose together in the morning, ate together, went to bed at the same hour, and talked little and with restraint; and when, as they sat from old habit together, the tension of their cool unquiet silence became too great, Emma would go off to find Dicky, or Lucia remember an unnecessary errand or take up—needlessly, like as not—some piece of work. And thus, with a visible half-sadness upon them, the old ladies came to be less than ever in their lives together; and winter lengthened towards spring; and with Emma now more than ever with him, Dicky stayed happily on.

In March, however, the good old lady fell ill again, and for three weeks saw the boy only in Lucia's presence in their bedroom. She talked to him, played games with him on the coverlet of her bed, read to him when she could; and often over some provocative passage in story or verse the young eyes met the old ones, and they had secret smiles in the silence that neither ever broke.

As she grew better again, though, and was able for slowly lengthening intervals to sit up in the sunshine, she noticed from day to day that the time he spent with her was diminishing, and sensed little by little the presence of something in him for which she couldn't satisfactorily account. The signs of it were the merest trifles—a lapse of his interest in what she read, in what she talked about—a frowning thoughtfulness for something within his own mind; but they were enough for Emma. He made, meanwhile, no mention of his preoccupation, and she, suspecting its character if not its theme, avoided the mistake of questioning him until they might talk of it alone. Thus it might almost have been her own question instead of his when, one day while Lucia was absent for a time from the bedroom, he a little impatiently asked how soon she would be well—be able to walk about again—and come to the nursery—and—and talk to him. Her answer was ready, and the way she made it was invitation enough for his straightest, fullest confidence—"Very soon I hope—perhaps this week. Why do you wish it so much?"

He crossed the room, looked into the hall, and then, with the door closed at his back, faced her for another moment's silence—serious, weighty silence—before answering—"I think I'm going away from here."

The expectant half-smile with which she had watched him passed now, and she answered in his own tone—"Going away?"

He nodded slowly—"With those children."

As his meaning—the meaning which was undoubtedly more than he knew—took form for her, Emma paled, and for seconds—in fact until he broke the silence again himself—she sat dumb, staring at him.

"Do *you*," he asked, "think they're happier than I am?"

"My dear child!" she at last found voice to exclaim, "whatever has put such a notion into your head?"

The small surprise with which he took this showed well enough that the notion was so familiar to him that he could wonder a moment at its newness for her; but briefly he went back a little into the month, empty for her, just behind them—"A new little girl—all grey—has come; the Dark Lady brought her. She thinks it's much nicer to be—to be the way they are, than to be the way I am. She wants me to be with them—like them."

Out of her amazement Emma's first clear impulse was to speak some sharp decisive remonstrance—but she restrained that, and, holding his eyes while she yet groped for the right thing to say, she merely dropped—"She is mistaken."

She saw then, however, by a slight deepening of the intentness of his look, that she was not to be let off with anything so simple as this—that she must amplify her statement in a measure she could now but half hopelessly guess the extent of; but there was no opportunity now, for before he could answer Lucia had opened the door and ushered in a maid carrying Emma's lunch. Her words were none the less, however, the key of the full answer she was to give him when, next day, as she sat in a wheel-chair in the nursery, they had taken up the question again—

". . . What I meant, my dear, is that the little Grey Girl is mistaken in thinking it much nicer to be as they are than as you are."

"Are you sure?" By the gravity of his doubt he might have been fifty instead of five.

But Emma had no smile for it—"I've thought of it half the night."

"But you know, Aunty, they do just whatever they want to; they never get hurt or sick or anything; and they go places; and nobody ever scolds them. . . ." His pause seemed only to indicate his groping for further desirable details, but she didn't wait for them—

"I know, Dicky, but you must remember that there are things—Oh so many things!—that you can do and have that they can't—that they can never have, now. You see, they'll always be the same—always and always—they'll never be anything but little children; but you'll grow up to be a man—a soldier perhaps; and shouldn't you rather do that than to—to go with them, and never be anything but a—just a—a—the kind of child they are?"

This argument, except for her hesitancy over definitions, had flown easily, as though its burden had been with her long before she spoke it—as if she had indeed thought of it half the night; but the haste of her words left them weak, and she could see by his silence, which indeed fairly bespoke a wish not to be convinced, that they had fallen short, that the impression she had to erase, the work she had to undo, had too firm and fixed a character to be thus so easily talked away. So, confused and worried, she was silent for a time; and his eyes rested expectantly upon her, and she wondered what to say next. She saw, too clearly now either to doubt or to discount, that from somewhere, by some means, he had got a view of a condition happier, in all ways better, than his own; she knew she must change that; and it turned over and over in her mind and nothing came to her that seemed worth saying, that seemed in the least to fit the occasion. What she wanted, what by quick intuitive good judgment she blindly groped for, was something better to offer him—something to outshine this Piper's promise—to glorify somehow the world he was in—to make him see the life he had and the life he faced as better, more beautiful and more alluring, than this featureless vision whose details she could neither see nor comprehend. But her memory, her imagination, her reason yielded for the moment nothing—nothing save a discouraging recognition of her incompetency to produce, in myth or fact, that right sufficient substitute. For who was she, she could but ask, to glorify life?—she, the horizon of whose existence had even in her forgotten youth encompassed barely more than it did at this hour, whose hopes, fears, experience, achievements had reached no farther than her garden wall, whose whole knowledge was but the fruit of a rigid childhood education, a proper magazine or two, a few dull books, the contacts of half-a-dozen people like herself. . . .

Meanwhile Dicky waited; and out of her anxiety she at last spoke again—made, to answer his half-certain doubts and convictions, an effort; for after all no mere disheartening measure of her shortcomings could alter her sense of the necessity of changing his mind—could silence the sinister persuasion of her uncertainty as to what might happen if she didn't—"You see, Dicky—yes, your little Grey Girl is wrong, quite wrong. If she knew of all the things you'd lose by—by going with her, I don't think she'd ask you. But she doesn't, my dear; she can't! She has never been anything but a child—a baby and a little girl, and what she is now; and if you do as she wants you to do you'll never be anything but a little boy—never be any bigger or wiser than you are now. You won't grow, you see—won't have any more birthdays. You won't go to school, never know how to read and write and draw pictures, never learn to whistle, never hammer another nail, never make another boat. *They* don't do these things, do they? . . . And all that is only for now; the important part is what comes later—what you would do—what you should miss—afterwards, when you should be a man."

His eyes, which had begun a moment ago to wander, had come back now, steady with attention, to hers, and, as to hold that interest, she drew him with one arm to her side, and went on more quietly, imagining as she went—"You know, outside—beyond our garden, beyond this town, beyond that city you used to live in—is the world—the great wonderful world that the poor little Grey Girl doesn't know anything about. No child as young as that, as small as that, could know very much about it. It is so big that you could ride in a train for days and days and only cross a small part of it, and when you had crossed that . . ." she paused for a second's thought, and then, half hopefully, half confidently, went on again—". . . when you had crossed that, you would come to the ocean—the beautiful, blue ocean . . . and then you would get on a great ship—grander than anything in your fairy tales—larger than this house—beautiful like a palace, and with engines in it to make it go. You would go to bed in that ship; think of it!—go to bed in a ship, and sleep there all night!—and next morning when you got up you would find yourself sailing away—with the sun shining on the water and the birds and white clouds in the sky and the great, great ocean all about. You would sail and sail—for days—and come at last to an island—a place with people living on it—and they would look at your wonderful ship and come up beside it in little boats and give you fruit—bananas, pineapples, good things to eat. But you wouldn't stop. You'd wave them good-bye and sail away from there; and after a while you'd come to another land—a great land this time, where you'd leave the ship and go into a city, full of people like you had never seen—brown people who always smile, and wear queer clothes. And they would put you into a little carriage with a man to pull it—to ride you through strange streets, where the houses are built of sticks and paper. And then . . . Oh, you would see wonderful things—white cities and black people, mountains, temples, strange trees, animals, little brown children who wear no clothes, men playing in the streets with snakes; you would ride long distances on the backs of camels—perhaps even upon elephants! And at last, after you had travelled weeks and weeks you would begin to see white people again, more and more of them; and you would ride in trains once more. You would see other cities, built hundreds and hundreds of years ago, where music is and beautiful pictures, and so many marvellous things to see and to do that you'd stay, perhaps, for a long long time. You'd see, too, a fairy city built in the sea, and magnificent churches, and castles, and marvellous mountains of ice and snow; and you would be in a city where you could see the palace of a real live king, and perhaps you would even see the king himself, riding in a golden carriage. And even if you didn't see the king, you could talk to his favourite soldiers, who are bigger than any man you ever saw and wear red coats and great black hats. . . . And at last you would get into another ship—like the first one—and that would bring you home—to your own country."

She stopped. Towards the last her words had come slower and slower; for sheer weariness her emphasis had dwindled; and her drop at the end had come too suddenly. But the look in the boy's eye had changed; she had caught his fancy, and the nimble little imagination, set dancing by her own first enthusiasm, would not accept the check—demanded some further demonstration of this successful trick she had been unable to play out to its end—"And my country—it's the best of them all, isn't it? What about *it*?"

Reading her advantage, as she couldn't indeed now fail to read it; fearful, moreover, lest she lose it, she tried courageously again—"Yes, my dear, it is certainly the best of them all, in so many ways that I can't begin to tell you . . . you must see for yourself, when you are a little bigger. It has oceans, your country—two of them—and lakes, great rivers, grand mountains; there are places in it where boiling water spouts straight out of the ground, where pools of water are that look like huge flowers, where rivers have made their pathways so deep and so beautiful that they can't be described, where the trees grow larger around than this room, higher than this house by many many times; it has cities—cities where trains run above the streets and under the ground. . . . Oh yes, Dicky, your country is wonderful enough; it's the place in the whole world where there's most to be happy about. And the boys who grow up to be men in it—men such as you would be, must be—do the most wonderful things—build cities and run railroads and . . . Listen—do you know what a factory is? Well, it's a place—a building, miles big—where things are done like in the Arabian Nights—where rocks are turned into iron, and iron is made into machines, where sheep's wool is turned into clothes, where trees become chairs and tables and beds and wood for our houses. . . . Shouldn't you like to see such wonderful things? shouldn't you like to *do* them? Well, you can, by staying—staying here with us—with me. . . . Your little Grey Girl, poor thing, doesn't know about these things at all; and if you went with her you wouldn't either. . . . And that would be a pity—a pity . . . a pity!"

There was between them for several seconds now only a thoughtful silence, and Emma, though sick and dizzy with fatigue, hardly able to sit erect in her chair, patiently did not break it. But he did at last, quietly—"You know, the Little Lady seems to think so too; she wants me to stay."

Still steadily, she eyed him a moment longer. "And what does the White Lady want? Isn't she anxious too?"

"No." He paused to consider. "She isn't *anxious*. She just seems to know I *will* stay—anyhow."

"Then you must! It is what we all wish, all of us who love you. It is best, Dicky—best!"

After this they said no more, and he wheeled her back to her bed. She managed to get into it, and then sent him off to find Lucia. But when Lucia came into the room and leaned close above the bed, Emma's closed eyes didn't open. Lucia turned to Dicky—"I guess," she whispered, "we won't wake her now."

VII

It was morning again then before the heavy lids of the sick woman lifted, before she saw Lucia, standing near the window and gazing out into the garden. Languidly, almost lifelessly, Emma watched her awhile, and then, wakening, noticed that the other bed was made, that the sun was already high, that it must already be late in the morning. Her eyes, widening now with a clear return of memory, came back to Lucia—"Sister!"

Lucia turned, approached the bed, said gently, "You've slept a long time. How do you feel?"

Emma raised herself, sat upright; and her lean back bent with weakness—"Better, I think. . . . Lucia, we ought to—we must—talk . . . about the boy."

But it was not until some care had been taken for the invalid's comfort—with basin, comb, breakfast, fresh bedding—that Lucia would consent to listen. Then Emma's first words, reaching back to their last sharp exchange over the child, struck straight—"You must write to Mary—at once. He must leave here." She paused a second; then—"He's in danger. Phoebe—wants him!"

Lucia's eyes, wide for one instant with astonishment, narrowed in the next with suspicion, and Emma, reading them, answered with scant patience—"Oh I'm not insane! He has seen her—and seen Milly, and Mary's mother. They've been visible to him for weeks—months . . . I assure you there can be no mistake, no 'falsehood,' about it!"

Lucia still eyed her in silence, but Emma's emphasis had been sure, and in her sister's look suspicion passed for a large uncertain wonder. Emma hurried on—"I'll not try to tell you everything now; but there are one or two . . . he saw Mary's mother first—during that time, you know? when he was so terribly lonely here? She came the first time alone, in the middle of the night; and then these children—she brought them, for companions—for him. The others—Phoebe and Milly—came later. Phoebe was standing in her own doorway. . . . He'd been playing, he says—running along the corridor—and suddenly noticed her standing there, watching him. He didn't know who she was, of course—though, Heaven help us, he appears to have known well enough *what* she was even then!—and he stopped to look at her. And then, before anything happened, Mary's mother appeared, and he noticed another—Milly—beckoning him away, towards the nursery. . . . Oh, it's terrible—terrible! . . . He says Phoebe is always trying to reach him—touch him; but Mary's mother . . . one is never there without the other; and even he, baby though he is, guesses their purposes—knows that Phoebe means him evil—that his White Lady is there to guard him! Well, she has managed so far to do it; but we mustn't leave it to her any longer! She still seems to dominate—"

"But please, please, Sister!" Lucia checked her. "Quiet, quiet! You know this is too—too extravagant. You can't be—I can't believe you're sure, really *sure*. Why, you speak as though they were actually here—alive—in the house! I'm afraid you've just been thinking about them too much; your memory of them is confused with something else—something you're afraid of. Don't you think so? . . . Now tell me, quietly, what you definitely know about them."

Emma, clearly confounded for the moment by this inability to see, could at first but look at her. Then—"Know?—*know!*—I definitely know exactly what I've just said!"

Lucia shook her head—"But how? How can you possibly know such things—about their relations—what they want—what they're trying—"

"From the child—from the child! *I* haven't seen them, Heaven knows; but *he* has—he does. He doesn't know who they are—or were; they're a White Lady, a Dark Lady, and a Little Lady, to him; but he describes them—by appearance, by behaviour, by character—down to the last habit: the White Lady tall, beautiful, 'queenly'—the Little Lady a small fidgety woman with a funny mouth—the Dark Lady a large black woman who knits—knits without needles—and watches him—always watches him. . . . Oh there are a hundred details, and we mustn't, we can't, doubt his evidence." She paused with this, but Lucia only continued to look at her. Emma went on more steadily, "The relations of the women, as I say, are very much as they used to be; and if there were no evil to fear but Phoebe herself I should be willing to go on trusting Mary's mother completely to cope with her. But that isn't all— that isn't all! Phoebe can be—or has been—kept away from him; but I learned only yesterday that she has brought a child (and perhaps there are a dozen by now!) of her own selection, and she, this child, can somehow reach Dicky where Phoebe can't. Don't ask me how it is; I can't tell you; I don't know. I only know that the boy is subject to that contact, and that it's dangerous. . . . It might almost as well be Phoebe herself! . . . At any rate," she wound up, letting Lucia have it now all at once, "he's already all but convinced that their existence, their state— dead or whatever it is—is a better one than his own; and this new child—this evil little agent of Phoebe's—has half persuaded him to—to join them. . . . Which means—"

She didn't finish, and as their eyes met and held now over her sudden silence, and as she sank back wearily into her pillows, Lucia's face changed with her decision, spoken the next minute as she got to her feet—"Well, I don't know—I don't understand; but I'll do as you say. I'll write to Mary—tell her what you've said. If you think best," she went on, "we'll move him out of the nursery. It will do no harm, anyway; and it would probably be well to have him sleep in here, with us."

*   *   *

An hour later, with Lucia gone—presumably to the library to write her letter—Dicky faced Emma, obviously with something to say. She had divined, during this half hour that he had been under her eyes, that there was something in his mind about which he was not at ease: a pensiveness, almost a sullenness, was upon him, and if it cleared occasionally, it was only to show him irritable. He had disapproved of this transfer from his room; his speech had been just too sharp, both to her and to Lucia; and, a rarity indeed for Dicky, there had been no smile on his face since they had summoned him. There was none now, as he faced her, and no gentleness in the voice with which, without a word from her in invitation, he stated, "They say you don't tell the truth."

Pain clouded her face, and a flash of indignation, but before these had passed for the look of hard concentrated interest with which she awaited whatever else he might have to say, she did coldly retort—"Then they're simply not telling the truth themselves."

But he paid, for the moment, no attention—"They're disappointed—the little Grey Girl and the others—(she's brought," he explained, "three others, just like her)—and the Dark Lady's mad! She heard you yesterday. . . . I wouldn't want her to be mad at *me!*"

"I shouldn't think," remarked the intent Emma, "you'd want to have anything to do with her at all."

His look, in the next silent second, seemed to say that what he wanted might have very little to do with it. But her sharpness had surprised him, evidently, as much as his own had seemed strange to her, and his next words came more softly—"Anyway, they say they have more to make *them* happy than those things you told me about. They say they don't need such things; they're just happy anyway, without them—happier than I'll ever be. Do you believe that?"

"Certainly not! Do you?"

As she held his eyes now, insisting a little mercilessly with her own that he answer, his face showed him unsure, and he looked away. She went firmly on—"What kind of children are these new ones, please? Are they like the others—like Beeba, and the little friends of the White Lady?"

He shook his head—"No; they're different."

"You don't like them as well, do you? They're not as nice, are they?"

His rebellious little firmness yielded a little—"No, they're not as nice."

She pressed him—"What have they done that makes you think they're not as nice?"

"Well—" he hesitated, thinking—"Well, they said things about the White Lady and the other children—and you. And they laugh—they made me laugh—at the Little Lady."

Emma took his hand, forced him to face her, to look at her, until the colour mounted high in his face. "It's exactly as I thought," she at last said; "they're simply bad children—bad, bad children! And if they're capable—if they are bad enough to be unkind about the White Lady, who has been so good to you, and about those other nice children, they're bad enough to tell lies too. And that is what they've done; they've lied to you. Now you mustn't listen to them any more. Not any more! You won't—will you?"

His eyes dropped again as he answered—"I promised them, though."

"Promised? Promised what?"

"What they want: to go with them—to be like them."

As he looked at her now his eyes, despite the guilt that still lurked in them, were steadier; the question, suddenly, was no longer of whether he was in the right, but of what should be done about his promise. But if it was a relief to him that the ground had thus so slightly shifted, she allowed him short enjoyment of it—"You had no right to promise, my dear, and you must think no more about it. You didn't even know," she went on, as to erase completely his obligation, "You didn't even know what you were promising."

He said nothing, but she could read in his face no acknowledgment of the finality she had sought; it demanded now some amplification of these last words of hers—seemed even to say that, firm, almost rough, as she had been with him, successful, even, as she had been with him, he still would take nothing unexplained, let nothing, if he could help it, go uncontested. Under other circumstances she must have admired his little staunchness; but she had no admiration for him now. She was already exhausted by these few hours' strain, by the excitement of this talk; twice in the last minutes she had lost him—lost everything—in a faintness that sickened and left her numb; and it was with an effort indeed that she sought now, with a feeble fierceness, to make her point— "Do you know that, to go with them—to be as they are—you would have to *die?*"

Her grasp, tight on his hand, drew him close to her, so that their faces were separate only by inches. His eyes widened and he tried to draw back, but she held him and rushed on—"To die, child—*die!*—leave me, and your daddy and your mother, who love you and need you—leave life, beautiful, wonderful life—that's what you'd have to do. Those wicked children—that terrible woman—are trying to kill you; do you understand?—to kill you! just to hurt your mother, hurt the White Lady— make them terribly unhappy. Would you like that? Would you let them do that?—let them hurt your mother? Would you—*would* you—"

She stopped suddenly, the passion in her face displaced by aston-ishment; for the child, with a sob of fear—fear of her—had broken roughly away and stood now apart, wide-eyed, staring at her as at some-thing horrible. . . .

And now at last she gave it up—relaxed—and as her eyes closed and she dropped back, tears—rare indeed for those eyes—slipped from between her lids. . . . But perhaps she had succeeded after all, for, after watching her a minute, Dicky came again to her side, touched her hand—"You scared me, Aunty; but don't cry. I won't do it—what they want. . . ." Her fingers closed weakly over his hand but her eyes didn't open, and she lay otherwise still as she answered—"That's a good boy, Dicky—a good boy."

Seconds passed then before either moved, and exhaustion and quiet lay upon one face and perplexity deepened in the other. Dicky broke the silence—"Aunty—"

Her voice was weak—"Yes?"

"But what shall I tell them?"

She made an effort—"It won't be necessary . . . you won't see them any more. We're going to keep you away from them."

He had no mercy—"You can't, Aunty. They go *any* place. They're waiting for me now, I guess, out in the hall. . . . I'm afraid of the Dark Lady. She'll be mad at *me* now!"

She looked at him, smiled, and the confidence of her reassurance, however extraordinary, was at least sincere—"Don't be afraid of her, my dear; the White Lady can keep her away from you. And the chil-dren—well, tell them something—anything . . . tell them I'll go, instead of you."

He returned her smile for the briefest uncertain instant, then frowned—"You?—instead of me? . . . Then *you'll* have to die!"

"Yes," she quietly answered; "and that would satisfy the children, I'm sure. And you mustn't mind, either. It's different, you see, with you and me. All those wonderful things I want you to do and see and know about—well, they're not for me now. I'm old—old; and soon I shouldn't be able to hear or see or be happy any more. Besides," she smiled again, "you remember how we decided that I'm not really necessary anyway—because Aunt Lucia is so much like me. . . . But that isn't so of you; you *are* necessary. It's—"

But she didn't finish. Her glance, attracted to a movement at the door, fixed itself there on the face of Lucia; and Lucia, with eyes that spoke she knew not what, stood looking at them until Dicky, following Emma's look, turned also to face her.

"Your lunch," she said to him, "is on the table. Come—I'll take you down."

A little reluctantly, and with a half-helpless last glance at Emma, he followed her; and when she returned a few minutes later Emma, without opening her eyes, said—"You heard us."

"Yes."

Each seemed, then, to wait for something from the other, until at last Emma spoke for both—"There seems to be nothing more to say. What shall we do?"

And Lucia, at the end of a second, could only answer, "I don't know."

Emma looked at her—"Well, if I were able to, I should take him straight from that lunch table out of the house—away—anywhere—never to come back!"

"Very well—but where?"

Emma wondered a moment—"How friendless we are! . . . Couldn't you ask the doctor?"

"The doctor's away."

Both were silent then until, as though the same thought had struck them at once, their eyes sought each other's. Emma suggested it—"There's that school—that Catholic place."

"Yes," said Lucia, and they still looked at each other. Finally she went on—"You don't object—you think it would be all right to take him there?"

"There's no place else."

"No—there's no place else. Well, I'll go and see them."

VIII

She had been gone nearly an hour when Emma, opening her eyes from a dark emptiness—a depth strangely deep for sleep—found herself, even in the first dimness of her awakening, thinking vividly, extraordinarily, of Milly—remembering the queer little face with a sharpness which by its startling life-likeness had, in an instant, cleared her consciousness with a shock and awakened her sharply to the sense of what, instead of sleeping, she should be doing. Lucia, after their decision, had brought Dicky back from the dining room and had then dressed and gone out, leaving the child under explicit injunction not to leave the bedroom. Emma recalled him now in a flash as deep in an afternoon nap in the middle of Lucia's bed; but in the instant it took her to turn her head to look for him she fairly turned cold. He was gone, and the bedroom door stood open.

A small bell lay within reach, and she seized it, rang it, repeatedly, frantically, until, after a time that seemed interminable, the scared face of the house-girl looked in at the door.

"Is Dicky downstairs? Have you seen him?"

But the girl hadn't—not since lunch time.

"Then find him—at once—and bring him straight here! Look— look in the nursery first."

Listening, she followed the heavy steps until, in the long carpeted hall, distance silenced them for her, and then, unable in her suspense to lie still, she sat upright, visualizing the girl's passage down the corri- dor—past the door that had not been opened for fifty years—past Phoebe's locked room before which Dicky himself had paused so often to wonder—past a last, extra room—and to the door of the nursery. . . .

Emma waited through another second's silence; then came faintly a sound like a far-off scream, the sound of someone running. She saw a figure—the servant's figure—rush past her own open doorway, heard her descend the stairs; and then heard only stillness.

In another second, barefoot, breathing in sobs, she was in the corri- dor, making her way on legs that would hardly support her, towards the nursery. The distance seemed to shorten by inches; in her weakness her limbs seemed lead-heavy; and she could feel the blood thumping loud and hard in her temples and neck and heart.

At the nursery door her legs gave way beneath her and she sank to the floor; and across the room, slumped down with his shoulders against the wall and his chin on his chest, lay Dicky. She called to him, got to her feet, stumbled, crawled, reached him, shook him, cried his name in his ear—then felt him stiffen, move a little—saw his eyes open and look at her. . . . At first, as though freshly wakened from a deep slumber, he didn't recognize her; then his arms went around her neck, held her tight, and she felt him sobbing. She held him, for sheer thankfulness, close against her a moment, and whispered, "Come, Dicky, quick— away from here."

He rose obediently enough, helped her to her feet; but as she stood erect the strength left her completely and she sank again, now into a chair—"Oh Dicky—I'm so sick . . ."

The boy looked at her in wide-eyed helplessness—"Aunty!— Aunty!—what shall I do?"

"Wait . . . I'll rest a bit. Look—isn't Lucia coming?"

He went to the window, but the walks outside were empty. Emma didn't move, but, as he watched, sat limp in her chair, her head in her hand, and waited. But something, perhaps only this silence—this charged silence—made the boy nervous—made him talk. His voice came to her as from a distance too great for any answer she could make to reach him; but she could hear—

"I didn't tell them what you said, Aunty—that you'd go instead of me; I didn't want them to have you. . . . But they knew it—they knew you said it, anyway . . . and they're going to take you all right—the Dark Lady is—if they don't get me."

She heard his step then, knew he had recrossed to her—was aware of him standing near—felt the pat of his hand upon her own, gentle, insistent. . . . She opened her eyes and looked at him—looked closer and almost with a start, into his face, which suddenly, amazingly, was not Dicky's face—not the face of the Dicky of yesterday, of this morning, of two minutes ago. The difference was not of a mere detail; this face was older; there was a grimness in it; the eyes were narrowed to slits and fixed with hard determination upon her own; and it was for that look, which was not of curiosity or fascination or mere interest, which searched for nothing, expressed nothing, but which seemed intent for no purpose but to *be* intent—it was for that look that she first found words to speak—"Why do you look at me like that?"

And even as he answered, his attention seemed less on what he said than on his purpose to hold his eyes unwaveringly still—"So as not to look at *them!*"

Her own eyes widened now—"Are they here?"

"They would be if I'd look at them—right there behind you, on the other side."

"The Dark Lady?"

"All of them—the new children. I'm not afraid of the Dark Lady; it's like you said—the White Lady keeps her away. But I mustn't, *mustn't* see those children! They— . . ." But now his voice seemed to dwindle, seemed far away—seemed to be coming from a distance which grew with sickening rapidity—widening . . . immeasurable . . . infinite. . . . His words were lost in a cold enveloping blackness . . .

. . . And now, as though hurtling towards her from that infinite remoteness, he came within earshot again and she heard him mention Lucia—understood that he thought he heard her in the house. As never yet, now, she struggled with this deadness—struggled to speak—to call out—fought her way up, like a deep-plunged swimmer, in the blackness that lay upon her . . . and only when her sister's step had sounded firm and unmistakable upon the nursery threshold did she relax and try no more.

*   *   *

Lucia stopped, just within the room, to look at them—at Dicky first, then at Emma with drooping head and hands upturned in her lap, and back again, sharply now, at Dicky. If her look was startled, fearful, it nevertheless remained fixed now for a second's growing astonished keenness for this pale sharpened little face, for these unnaturally narrowed little eyes now fixed with a determination almost desperate upon her own, for the irresistible quivering of this little lip, for the pathos of this plea—

"Please take me away!"

She hesitated, glanced at Emma—"There's a man waiting for you downstairs—in the parlour—"

She stopped. Dicky's eyes had suddenly gone shut—tightly, intentionally shut—and with hands raised and trembling he was groping his way towards her. The hard little courage had melted; his face, with the approach of tears, had wholly changed; and in another second, helplessly crying, he had found her, seized her dress, buried his face in it—"I can't—can't—go alone, Aunty—I can't go alone. . . ."

Taking his hand then she led him, sobbing, from the room, down the corridor, the stairs—where his steps were cautious and his free hand followed the banister. If she wondered why his eyes kept shut she didn't ask, but still silently held his hand—until it had passed to that of the waiting priest, who may have wondered too. She took them to the door—watched them across the veranda and down the walk—saw Dicky look up at his companion. . . .

And meanwhile, upstairs in the nursery, Emma hadn't moved—hadn't fallen. The head still heavily drooped, the hands lay still upturned in her lap. . . .

Part 4
The Lady who wished

As a case of feeling—of crushing, bewildering emotion—the experience from which her unusual wish had emerged had been, for Lucia, at some points tremendous—more so, doubtless, than she knew. She knew indeed, and gratefully, very little about it—recalled with certainty only that it had begun with the death of Emma—had drawn its black unhappy progress through an unbearable grief, through collapse, delirium, illness—and had lost its severity at last in a vague half-blankness, like a troubled interminable sleep, from which she had awakened to the beginning of recovery. But if she was thus vague—and altogether willingly so—about her illness, she took in contrast a more than compensating interest in certain striking features of its consequence—features whose purport, faintly suggested in the first clear quiet of convalescence, had soon become unmistakable, had here and there considerably surprised her, and had ended by convincing her that her improvement amounted to something rather more than mere recuperation—included, comfortingly, some permanent and altogether happy details of change.

Of the detectable items of difference, some of which indeed were but faint and elusive at best, two were quite, were increasingly, distinct: one, a wholly unfamiliar emotional quiet—a pleasant all-prevalent indifference which reduced to unimportance literally everything in the world; and the other, more striking still, having to do with her memory and imagination—or rather, with an unfamiliar, delightful faculty in which memory and imagination were at moments indistinguishably mixed, and which made thinking a rich, sometimes almost a thrilling pleasure—gave to the devised fictions of her brain the clearness and authority of memories, and lent to things remembered a vividness strangely like reality. . . .

No doubt it was natural that of the whole change she should find these two features, of her complacency and her imagination, quite the pleasantest. But Lucia liked them all—liked, while it lasted, the mild excitement of discovering and examining them—liked them for the things they excluded or replaced—liked above all the ultimate important use to which the best of them could be put. Naturally—inevitably—this use, upon which she seized, and which she lovingly cultivated, was to enlarge, to enhance, to give the greatest attainable clearness and completeness to, everything she remembered or felt or fancied with regard to her beloved and unforgettable Emma; and if her mind—a chamber stripped, as it were, of its old trappings and illuminated now with unaccustomed light—if her mind could no longer willingly content itself with the plain concerns of her household, that difference at least provided a space the greater, a range the wider, for the play of this freer, fonder interest.

While, however, this coincidence of interest and its means of ministration was, so far as it went, of the happiest, the action of the means was distinctly not invariably pleasant. There were times, indeed, when the things it did for her—the sharpness of memory it brought, the prodigies of fancy it produced—quite reached the extreme of what she could comfortably bear. And always, of course, even at its best, it must in a measure fail of ultimate adequacy . . . in spite of it—in spite of anything and everything—the emptiness she strove to make it fill remained at last still too deep, too great! She yet, however, hungrily clung to it, used it, developed it: it came nearer than anything else to yielding what she so deeply needed; and if it fell to an inordinate memory thus at the beginning sometimes to wound her with abnormal revisionings, it was to become the office of an equally inordinate imagination in the end to turn them, in restitution, to another account—to select, to reshape, to interpret every adaptable passage in the history of her house, first to foster an extraordinary wish, and at last to sustain a strange unearthly hope. . . .

For hadn't Katherine, for a sufficient reason and on more occasions than one, prodigiously returned?—and hadn't Phoebe?—and Milly?—and even, in her own childhood, that uncle . . .? And if they had, why not Emma?—why not Emma? Except for the uncle, Lucia didn't know—really *know*—that they had; indeed, she had always before disbelieved it as firmly as she could. But she didn't want to disbelieve it any longer. She wanted—needed—to believe it; and she found in time most wonderfully that she could—found it easy to accept this possibility which had once seemed monstrous, and to accept it at last even as the subject of the deepest, the only, hope she cared to keep.

I

Her unconcern with regard to other things in which she might well enough have had an interest was fairly exemplified, some weeks after she had left her bed, in her reaction to the death of Mrs. Stroub. With the doctor, Lucia sat at her old friend's bedside and, without a pang worth the name, watched her die. Afterward, bidding the doctor good-bye, she remarked with just a touch of sadness—"And now we two— you and I—are all that are left . . ." and that, as an expression of what she felt, was all.

The doctor's answering calmness was—though perhaps for another reason—quite the match of her own—"Yes." And his next words, accompanied by a look professionally direct into her face, might well have been chosen for their lack of sentiment—"She'll be hard to replace, won't she. Have you thought of that?"

Lucia a little blankly shook her head—"There has hardly been time. . . . I suppose I'll have to have someone. . . ."

"Yes, you'll have to have someone," he promptly rejoined. And then, a bit brusquely—"If you'll let me, I'll select her for you."

"Well—if you would. . . ."

So he did. And when, not a great while later, the woman he had chosen announced to Lucia that the doctor himself was dead, she took the information with a long look into this new face—the look, clearly, of a woman thinking of something else—and answered absently, "—so that everyone—quite everyone left alive now—is a stranger."

"Aren't you," the housekeeper suggested, "forgetting your niece?"

Lucia shook her head—"They're too remote. Children, all of them—and so infinitely far away. . . . Besides, they mustn't come here."

*   *   *

So far as her indifferent attention troubled itself to observe, the doctor's selection of a housekeeper had evidently been excellent. Lucia didn't know her very well—saw her occasionally, spoke to her little, remembered her indistinctly as a large, composed, grave woman who had in their first interview eyed her with uncalled-for keenness and demanded a higher salary than Mrs. Stroub had had. Lucia had wondered a little at first just what to expect of her—just how much of the household supervision, so long wholly in her and Emma's hands, she wanted to surrender to a stranger. But if Lucia had been uncertain, the stranger evidently hadn't—had indeed so demonstrated her certainty that before very long the management of the house was quite a forgotten concern for its mistress. She was vaguely aware that changes had been made in its long-established program; but she complacently didn't bother about them. There was really no need—no need to bother about such things, nowadays, in the least. If she forgot to order the groceries, they were ordered anyway; if she failed occasionally in the life-long habit of making her own bed, it was nevertheless beautifully ready for her at night; if, even, she overlooked the hour of meal-time, somebody unfailingly remembered to remind her. . . .

In her personal schedule, meanwhile, the fixed items consisted mainly of a little sleep, a great deal of thinking, a hobby for mirrors, and a habit of walking, literally for hours every day and often enough in the night as well, through the house. She had been dimly aware at first that this last—this tireless wandering from room to room, from the top of the house to the bottom, through the halls, the kitchen, the library, the nursery—might seem odd; but she secretly considered its purpose too important to be slighted on that account. It was in Lucia's view no mere idle habit of walking about; it was a means of anticipation—the best way she knew, simply, of guarding against the failure of being wherever it should be necessary, to meet what it was she more and more deeply forever hoped for.

The game of the mirrors—odd too, defensible too—was the result of her having, while absorbed one day in some recollection of Emma, caught unexpectedly a full view of her own reflection in their bedroom glass. For the instant her wish, her hope, were in effect fulfilled—and with a pleasure whose pitch and thrill were like nothing else she had ever experienced—were, in any case, by all means worth seeking again. . . . So, in abundant provision for that possibility, she had fairly dotted the avenues of her wanderings with the responsive faces of mirrors.

The trick had been to a degree successful—until, as she grew familiar with their positions, the delicious unexpectedness of their effect was more and more often lost. She had them redistributed; and when, after a short time, the second arrangement failed like the first, she asked her housekeeper to change them again—to relocate them however she might wish. . . . The woman hesitated, not wholly sure, evidently, of her mistress' intent—"You want them arranged, as they are now, all over the house, but in different places?"

"Yes; just wherever you wish—only put them, as much as you can, everywhere—wherever I walk."

"I see. But I hope," the housekeeper smiled, "that you won't mind if you discover them in some rather unexpected places."

Lucia laid a long hand on her wrist—"I shan't mind that at all, my dear. . . . In fact the unexpectedness is—is what I most want."

But though she got it—though the ingenuity of her housekeeper rendered the illusion in some measure readier and easier than it had yet been—that too, before long, proved not enough. It remained after all an illusion—recurrently thrilling but recurrently disappointing, and with a limitation precisely as marked as the perimeters of the mirrors themselves. And so, before the persuasion of her wish, her hope, her determination almost, she tried then not to know them as mirrors at all—began the practice of speaking to her image, of reaching out tentatively, timidly, to touch it. If it faintly occurred to her that this was going rather far, she could for answer reflect that this silent game might deceive her as readily in the wrong direction as it had so pleasantly done in the right—that should she happen—*should* she happen—to meet what she sought, the response to a spoken word, to a voluntary touch, would doubtless be of itself all the longed-for evidence she should require. And at last, even while her sole distinguishable reward still amounted to no more than the reflected motion of her lips and the coldness of the glass against her fingers, there grew upon her the sense of a difference not visible—not palpable ... but faintly, insistently sure. ...

She couldn't have told how it began, couldn't have told even in what it consisted, except that it seemed to have come not so much from without as from within herself—seemed more than anything else simply a matter of her own sense of a deepening strangeness in her deception. She tried, tried hard, tried sensibly and practically, to explain it—attributed it to her housekeeper's success in arranging her mirrors for the unexpectedness she had sought, to some illusive effect of light or position, to her own states of mind; but these, she soon saw, had nothing to do with it. It was too distinctly a thing of itself—a thing, in time, of constantly clearing identity and emphasis. An early effect of it was to alter the manner of her speaking to her image—to change it from the coolly conscious experiment it had at first been to the expression of pure hopeful impulse; it was a striking consciousness of it on some later occasions that made her forget to speak at all; and it was a startling flash of it—a wave of feeling too strong not to leave a conviction of some real significance for the difference—that sent her back one day, bewildered and half afraid, from an encounter in a hallway nook to her bedroom to analyze her feelings—to adjust her thoughts—to decide just what had happened. ...

She had been walking towards the steep remote stairway to the attic, and on turning into the short hall passage lying at its foot, had been confronted with the spectacle of a full-length figure resembling herself. In this program of hope, of hunger, of make-believe, these images were to

Lucia of course always, for a second, those of Emma; but where the illusion so often lasted but an instant, or at most for a rigid half-dozen seconds, this experience today had been in the extreme different—had had no air of illusion about it, no suggestion of the familiar dissolution of a thrilling first impression into an undeceived second one—but, striking her at once with its semblance of reality, had deepeningly continued to impress her so for as long as she had been able to face it. That had not, she was soon to see, been long enough: the scene hadn't been rightly, fully concluded; she had wavered, had turned aside, had bewilderedly left the corner, strangely numb and strangely excited, and with a persistent sense of being followed by the eyes of that figure whose features and stature, whose shadows and dead colours, so closely resembled her own. Its details returned readily enough to her mind—some familiar ones, of their general similarity, to be disregarded, and certain others quite necessarily not to be—a sallowness and thinness of face, for one thing, just perceptibly more pronounced than her own, and, more striking still, a simple and far less easily explicable matter of a bit of lace. . . .

Weeks before, because they were badly worn, she had removed from the wrists of her dress their bits of trimming; and because it was but too easy nowadays to neglect such unimportant things, she hadn't since replaced them. But that other dress, in other details so like her own, had differed in this: its wrists were properly trimmed with lace.

She sat for some time quite still, waiting deliberately until she should be calm again, and reconstructing meanwhile as completely as she could the scene and the sense of what had just taken place. She remembered readily enough her actions—her approach, her startled recognition, her long still stare, her retreat; but it was considerably less easy to recall how she had felt. . . . There had been something of a shock, a kind of emotional numbness, a faint, half-blank confusion. She wondered why she hadn't, as she had so long and so confidently supposed she should, felt some high pulse of pleasure—and if not that, why there had been nothing of fear—of the sense, after all but too readily possible, of the horrible. . . . At any rate she had felt neither—had been neither definitely glad nor definitely afraid—had been more than anything else only speechlessly surprised; and as she sat now contemplating that plain result her disappointment in it steadily deepened. She blamed, of course, herself—saw it not only as regrettable but as clumsy, almost as stupid—to have felt and acted so—to have done nothing, said nothing, thought nothing, when of all times she should have thought and spoken and acted with the highest, clearest precision!

But at last, when resolutions of what she should do on the occasion of the next encounter had begun already hopefully to take shape in her mind, it chillingly dawned upon her that she might have been mistaken—that what she had seen, what she had been unable to face, might after all have been nothing but her own reflection. . . . She returned to the spot to see.

Passing along the corridor, consciously, carefully calm, she decided upon what, this time, must be done. Whatever she should encounter must be met quietly, and must be met, moreover, with the clearest perception and the gentlest speech and action of which she was capable. She would of course look first for a mirror—be sure it was, or was not, there. If she found one, there would be nothing to do but scrutinize her reflection in it very thoroughly; if she didn't find one, she should wait a little; if she found anything else, she must show no excitement, no distress, no alarm—she must speak, simply, a gentle greeting. . . .

Coming to an abrupt halt at the angle of the wall beyond which lay her destination, she saw within its shadow exactly—quite to the last detail—what she had seen there half an hour before. For a second—for two, five, ten seconds—she merely rigidly looked; and then, for eagerness, for doubt—to confirm or to refute the full prodigious suggestion of what she saw—she began determinedly to measure, to make sure of, its details—of its slight difference from herself in length and colour of face, of the lace trimmings upon these other sleeves, of the peculiar fixity of these other eyes whose expression of quiet contemplation was surely no reflection of her own mounting excitement. . . . But after a minute she couldn't continue, couldn't scrutinize—forgot her plans—forgot to look for a mirror; the urge, swelling almost fiercely in her mind, to verify in some way this thing she could helplessly neither believe nor disbelieve of her eyes, to confirm somehow else, somehow better, this visual realization of her wish, suddenly, irresistibly prevailed . . . and perhaps no burst of questions, nothing she could have thought of to say or to do, could have carried better the burden of what she strove to know than the half-audible single word that then escaped her—"Emma!"

Without knowing—without wondering—how, and before the word could have echoed from the nearest wall, she found herself possessed of all the answer her hungry wonder had need of. It was full and sharp and richly positive; it had come without sound, without gesture—but as it flashed upon her, as she grasped and held it, the wonder of how it had come was lost in the greater, happier wonder of what it brought. For that—what it brought—was in the broadest sense the realization of her hope: the certitude, unconfused and vividly clear, that at last this circumstance for which she had so deeply, so intently longed, this gift of sight and communication, this prodigious fact of repossession, had indeed become, from mere imagined possibility, a now forever unquestionable item of experience.

And so for some seconds—seconds in which her excitement, the high intensity of her interest, reached its peak, passed, gave place to a deep absorbing quiet—they stood motionless, speechless, and with eyes unwaveringly fixed across the dusk . . . until, with a sudden barely perceptible softening of its face, a slow tentative soundless forward step, the figure had halved the distance between them. Lucia quietly smiled; and if her calmness seemed to betoken a poor appreciation for the full unanswerable significance of that step, it was not that the significance was lost—it was merely, beautifully, that she didn't, now, need it.

It dawned upon her then suddenly and quite definitely that the experience had gone sufficiently far—that, for the moment, she had had enough. She felt herself all at once ever so slightly oppressed with weariness, felt the relaxation of the next second a change indeed—vaguely, pleasantly irresistible—from the tension which had preceded it—and turned away, strangely without further concern for Emma, but strangely certain that this hour's experience marked, for something far, far richer, merely the beginning.

II

How well founded this certainty was, the next day and the next and those that followed, with their cumulative confirmatory succession of view and contact and communication, were sufficiently to show. They had next met, on the following day, in the hallway before the nursery door, had stood for a long moment looking at each other—Emma gently and seemingly without intent, Lucia, after a second's half-credulous stare, with clear pleased composure; they had walked thence together, without communication and quite as though it were altogether the natural thing to do, to their own room, and had entered; and then Emma, after a brief full wistful survey of its contents, had turned away and passed again into the corridor. Lucia, calmly and still silently watching her go, had sat down then to think the scene over—to review the expressions, the movements, the clear significant completeness of all its action—to be pleased with its simplicity—to be impressed last and most with its quiet convincing naturalness. . . . The next occasion—on which Emma had come to her late at night in the downstairs parlour, and had led her, pleasedly compliant, to bed—had been yet easier; and so, subsequently, had each been as it came. And as they became more frequent, less tentative, and of ever lengthening duration, they lost by degrees the quality of strangeness. What had begun by being prodigious became all but usual; it came to be the common thing for these two to meet, to walk, to sit together; and Lucia's days and evenings and nights were at last no longer empty.

There pleasantly remained, though, one feature of their association to which she didn't for a long time become just complacently accustomed. This was the manner of their communication; and even after weeks of familiarity with it, when she had learned gratefully to take so much else almost as matter of course, this one particular seemed quite as remarkable as ever. . . . Her own part in their exchanges consisted, of course, simply in the natural spoken utterance of her thoughts; but the manner in which she received those of Emma was hardly so usual! Not that there was any difficulty about it—no dribbling continuity of words, no clumsy ineptness of expression—no sensible transitional means at all: rather, and in the most beautifully easy way in the world, it seemed that whatever Emma had for her did not understandably so much pass from one to the other as simply suddenly to *be* there, clear and complete, in her consciousness—as though, by an action like nothing so much as a pulse of intuition, the products of that other mind became the possessions of her own.

She could of course recall that it had been a little like this before—long in the past, when their living sameness had had so strikingly the effect of lessening their need for speech; but she remembered nothing of the kind so vivid, so nearly perfect, as this. She had never during that time, as she often did now, asked triflingly idle questions for the pure joy of receiving their answers; more surely still, she had never then known anything approaching the pleasure that Emma's unprovoked and unexpected communications held for her now. And this not because of the substance, the jewel-like clearness, of the thoughts themselves; the sensation of receiving them was what she liked—the stimulus, the sharp inward tremor that their sudden presence invariably excited. She couldn't explain it; she didn't try; she was satisfied simply to know it, and to wonder at it, as a feature of the broadening, the ever more inclusive, pleasure of this comradeship—the pleasure to every shade and substance of which she clung with conscious fondness—and which she at moments gravely felt she should now never again be able to do without. . . .

As their association grew, meanwhile, there but naturally developed with it its peculiar schedule. When she awoke in the morning and sat for a few minutes on the edge of her bed to avoid the dizziness of standing too suddenly, Lucia's long white feet sought her slippers in their accustomed places, and her eyes sought Emma. Usually they found her at the window—quite as though she had risen earlier and already dressed; and, as their eyes held for a second, Lucia would speak a quiet good-morning. Later, washed and refreshed, when she had unbraided her single thin plait of hair, and sat erect and lean in her white gown before the dresser, her glass of hot water would arrive from the kitchen. The delivery of this drink, in the hands of a half-embarrassed house-girl, was always an occasion for amusement—an occasion on which she watched the girl with smiling silent curiosity, wondering whether, today, she would "see"—and invariably she and Emma could exchange a smile over the fact that she didn't. . . . When she was dressed she made, from old unconscious habit, a quick comparative scrutiny of their appearances, and then went downstairs to breakfast. Emma usually remained behind, or at most went with her only to the stairs. . . . After breakfast for an hour or two, or for the entire morning, they would be together again—in inspecting the house, in merely sauntering through it, or, as Lucia often chose, in silent idleness; in the afternoon she slept—so that their nights, spent usually in the downstairs parlour, might be a little longer; and in the small hours of the morning she went to bed. Emma stayed with her while she undressed, while she braided her hair and rubbed cold cream into her face and hands, while she said her prayers; and when the light was out Lucia's last consciousness before she dropped to sleep was of the dim familiar figure facing her from a chair before the window. She liked this picture best when there was a moon to make its outlines clear, to make of its colours a blend of pallor and grey and thin soft silver . . . but she had noticed that light—extraneous light—need not, necessarily, shine. . . .

Their hours downstairs at night constituted, for Lucia, the most important—altogether the richest and most satisfying—part of their association. She liked it, for one thing, because of the quiet, because of the completeness of their possession of the scene. Moreover, so much of their lives had been spent in this room—in their last years alone, before that when Milly and Mary had been with them, and yet further back, when Phoebe and Katherine had had places in its lamplight—that it seemed now but the natural theatre for this partial recovery of that experience. They did, in these nights, but the simplest things: Lucia knitted, read the Bible, wrote to Mary or read for the twentieth time her letters; and Emma merely watched her, or moved about the room, or gazed out of the windows or into the fire as she had used to do. Their talk led them, but naturally, much into the past—turned upon their sisters, their youth, the changes that had come. And what tremendous changes they seemed!—how far, far different the facts and the action of their last thirty years from the calm promise of their first fifty! They dwelt much upon the first fifty—upon the time before Katherine had come, when they had had still their brother Emerson, when Phoebe had sat here with them, when Milly had amused and interested and shocked them with her gossip. . . .

It occurred to Lucia more than once, and increasingly as something of a pity, that it could not all—the *whole* association—be brought back. And because she liked the notion, because the charm of its prospect steadily increased for her, she suggested it to Emma, specifying, "—but just ourselves, Sister—you and Phoebe and Milly and I—as we were at first, when we had only ourselves to think about." And if she noticed that Emma's response reflected none of her own enthusiasm, the observation didn't especially reduce the pleasure she took in imagining that complete reunion. Nor did it prevent, later on, her experimental, anticipatory gesture of placing the chairs of the two missing sisters in their old accustomed places—Phoebe's near the light, Milly's in her corner—and of laying an unfinished piece of knitting in the one and a novel from the little lady's bedroom in the other.

If there was any unnaturalness, any queerness, about this, about anything they did, Lucia had by now long since lost that sense of it; it had come to seem, all of it, more natural than not: the morning greetings, the walks, the talks, these nights together, this high dim room with its ancient carpet, its fire-place, its grim furniture forced hard against the walls, its bits of lonely looking porcelain . . . this was all quite as it ought to be—quite as it had always been; and Lucia, occupied with a letter at the desk in the corner, or facing the fire from the chair she had sat in for sixty years—there was nothing unnatural, certainly, in that. As for Emma—well, the chair she used was no less hers than was Lucia's her own, nor the movements she made, nor her air, her attitudes, her look. And the things they talked about were the old, the customary, things—little commonplaces of the house as it had been, the old-time order, the old-time servants, their own habits, their memories. . . .

But of course, for Lucia, this question of mere usualness was of little importance anyway. What she had, what Emma's return had wonderfully wrought, amounted to a re-establishment of part of the order which had yielded all the interest, all the happiness, of her life; and that its features presented to her so little the face of strangeness was not, as she viewed it, a great matter. What she saw before anything, what she was unable to forget, what for her transcended every question of oddity or fact or truth, was the simple wonder of the comradeship itself—which, in her own conviction, could but mean for all that remained to her of life the security of a beloved companionship—which entitled her to hopes, to interests, to a gladness that nobody understood, that she expected nobody to understand, and whose cause she cherished like a treasure—like a sacred secret.

*   *   *

If their interest and their talk seemed very largely for the past, however, it was yet not entirely so. There were still the children—Mary, Richard, Dicky—if not to hold them in the present, at least sometimes to bring them interestedly back to it—as they were brought back indeed one day on the receipt of a letter from Mary. . . .

Lucia, saving it until the night-time, had brought it into the parlour, had opened it and read aloud its first few sentences, and then, with changing face, had hurried on through it in silence. When she had finished, had looked for some seconds, vaguely troubled, into Emma's face, she stood up and laid the letter on the table between them—"They're coming back to America."

Emma's response was long in coming, and when it came it but echoed the question which Lucia herself had already in the silence blankly, half-fearfully faced—"Are they coming here?"

Lucia could do no better for her sister than she had been able to do for herself—"Do you think they should?"

The answer, its sense unmistakable, came with shocking suddenness, with an effect as of harsh and unexpected sound—

"Well, they *shall* come here!"

—but it was distinctly not an answer of Emma's; and Lucia, whirling to face the spot whence it had come, found herself looking into the eyes of Phoebe. For a long moment she didn't move, and when at last she did it was only to turn, dumb and helpless, back to Emma. And Emma, with never so much as a glance for Phoebe, but with a face grave and troubled for Lucia, slowly shook her head.

Lucia continued standing, motionless, soundless, unthinking; and in the stillness her look fixed steadfastly, as for refuge, on the face of Emma. And then, behind Emma in the dimness of a far corner, she noticed a movement—noticed a figure with fingers fidgeting at its mouth, with eyes shifting from one to another of her sisters' faces. . . . But beyond a faint fleeting surprise of recognition, this new presence—Milly's presence—made no difference—touched not at all, at any rate, this other, deeper, concern; and Lucia's eyes returned in a second or two to the waiting face of Emma.

She saw no solution, no suggestion, there. . . . But they—she and Emma—had never openly opposed Phoebe, and this moment's bewilderment held for her neither the intention nor the courage to do so now.

She turned again to look at Phoebe, and again looked worriedly away—going, this time, to sit down near Emma. Phoebe's eyes followed her; and a little later, with face unchanged, she too took her old accustomed chair.

III

It was, in some sense, what she had wanted, what her wished-for restoration of the conditions of their complete familiar past had contemplated. But as she sat now in the midst of its but too sufficient evidence—sat, in hurt confused silence, looking steadily, for composure, into her lap—it was hardly to be glad for this fulfilment—was at last far less to take the measure of what she had gained than sinkingly to take that of what she had not! For as she had conceived it, dwelt upon it, talked of it to Emma, this return had admitted always only themselves—her sisters, their interests, the interests of a period exclusively their own; and it was exactly that precious exclusion that she had missed—that the bitter purpose of Phoebe seemed decisively, finally, to preclude. Phoebe had not returned, as Emma had, to comfort her—not simply, as she had wished, that they might all be together again "by themselves"—but in a relation charged through and through, charged wrongly, inimically, dangerously, with the concerns of somebody else. Mary, Mary's husband, Mary's son, held their place high enough in her affections; but it was, had inevitably always been, a place apart; and that late far-reaching wish of hers, in this moment so portentously realized, had considered them not at all—had less than anything, certainly, considered them threatened with such a contingency as this!

*   *   *

If she had a little fearfully shrunk, in that first hour, from the contemplation of what that contingency amounted to, it was none the less disquietingly with her, demanding recognition, requiring the clearest consideration, the most intelligent judgment, she could give it, on the morrow and for days following—days in which worry shadowed her as it had not done for months, in which the delicately pleasant little vaguenesses of her life dwindled and vanished, in which the close pressure, the dark significance, of Phoebe's presence would let her think of nothing else. What went on now in the kitchen or the laundry or the garden were forgotten indeed, and so, oftener than ever, the hours of her meals, the names and faces of her servants, the simple concerns of her personal care and dress and habit. . . .

In contrast, the figures and conditions of what she was unable to forget but grew in vividness. If mere visible resemblance had been enough, surely she could have found, in this reflection of their past, no faintest reason for complaint. . . . But even as she took in, in the still night-time of the parlour, the features of this resemblance—as she wonderingly measured its completeness, its clearness, its accuracy—saw again her sisters, to the last detail of appearance and habit as they had lived, felt again the forces of their so different personalities, learned again the meanings of their looks, the tones of their moods—she must yet helplessly see beyond them—must yet sinkingly, fearfully remember the hovering dark failure of their restoration. And glancing aside from the fire she could read Emma's sympathy for her disappointment, could see Milly in the corner watching her, watching them all, wondering what was going to happen. . . . And Lucia could not but wonder too.

She had, at all events, carefully permitted nothing to happen on that first night, but had gone at the end of half an hour abruptly to bed, leaving Phoebe and Milly, and taking Emma with her. Next night, entering the parlour at eleven o'clock, she had found them awaiting her—and had had courage enough to meet the steady inquiring look of Phoebe, and to speak some greeting. By the fourth night it had seemed to her that the tension had lessened a little—or, if it hadn't, that there was at least no longer any question of her being able to put up with it until it did. But two nights later, on the strained stillness of their gathering,. with harsh and startling suddenness, the question struck—

"Are they coming?"

Lucia faced her questioner—"No."

The first response to this, continuing through minutes of silence, was merely the change in Phoebe's face—the change from its hot hard look of inquiry to the old familiar mask of anger. And at last—"But *I want* them!"

Bravely, Lucia tried to say the things which in the last six days she had decided to say—"They all understand, Sister—that is, I've repeatedly urged them not to come—never to come here again. It's hardly—it's—it's impossible—"

"*No!*" Phoebe had risen; and poor Lucia could but fearfully watch the great old figure, the never-to-be-forgotten lines and distensions and quiverings of its face, advance towards her. Dimly she knew that Emma was up, had come to her side; and something like a whimper—Milly's old whimper—seemed to sound for her as from a great distance. . . .

But then abruptly, as by a changed decision, Phoebe stopped, turned away, and with no sideward look passed with her old ponderous slowness through the door and out of sight in the direction of the stairway.

For three nights following, then, there was peace—except, for Lucia, for the persistent troubled uncertainty of the future. It strengthened her resolution somewhat for the moment that both Emma and Milly acknowledged her opposition as the only right action, for Mary's sake, to have taken; and Emma's encouragement, especially, helped her to the selection of the line she was to take with Mary herself—the means by which she was to keep that distant small family, as she so distinctly felt she must keep them, out of her house. . . .

Her letter, already long, was yet unfinished when, suddenly aware of someone near her, she looked around to see again the figure of Phoebe. It towered just behind her, and its eyes which were not for her searched with an eager frowning curiosity the half-filled sheet that lay upon the desk. What Phoebe saw there was evidently of no very distinct significance to her, for after a moment her eyes left the paper for Lucia's face, without satisfaction, without anger, without apology—expressing, if they expressed anything, only an almost anxious curiosity. Lucia faced her for a second, looked undecidedly back at her writing, dipped her pen as though to go on, and then, with cold courage, laid down the pen, placed the unfinished letter in a drawer, and closed the desk. Phoebe, she meanwhile knew, hadn't moved; and now, looking again into the stern old face Lucia saw there only a hard, displeased perplexity—at once the mystification and her distaste for it as to what this hesitancy, this concealment of the unfinished letter, meant.

But if it took, on Lucia's part, some courage thus to leave her in the dark, surely it would have taken a great deal more not to; and she simply didn't, at this point, have it. She returned, however, deliberately enough to her chair—and, until she went to bed, remained there in uneasy consciousness of the searching uncertainty of Phoebe's gaze. She affected to ignore it—gave assiduously her attention to Emma—and meanwhile firmly determined to finish her letter somehow—anyhow—in the morning.

When, however, she returned next day, straight from the breakfast table, there, in the chair before it and helplessly gazing at the closed desk, sat Phoebe. Lucia paused, started to turn away; but Phoebe had seen her, and if the heavy old face expressed no trace of welcome it did undeniably at least betray a hopeful expectation. Confused and disappointed, Lucia paused but long enough to speak a word of greeting, and passed on to her fireside chair. Here, with her back squarely towards the figure whose eyes she knew well enough had not left it, she sat for only a moment—for perhaps just too short a moment; and then, with a pale strained smile for her companion, and a step just too suggestively decisive, she left the parlour. . . . If it had amounted to a disadvantage that

Phoebe's curiosity had kept her here, guarding this desk, for twelve hours, it amounted none the less now to a possibility not to be ignored that it might do so for twelve more. . . .

But twenty minutes later, as she sat hurriedly writing in her bedroom, a motion of Emma's directed her attention towards the door; and there, narrowly eyeing them, Phoebe was just entering. Disconcerted and a little scared, Lucia shuffled what she had written beneath a blank sheet, and stood aside. Phoebe advanced slowly round the foot of the bed and to the table, scanned for a second the clean paper upon it, and then, unsatisfied, and turning her eyes again upon Lucia, sat down between the twins to wait. Lucia looked at her, looked at Emma, turned away and crossed to the window, and, at the end of ten uncomfortable minutes, discouragedly left the room.

If she had been mistaken a short time ago in supposing that Phoebe would remain indefinitely on guard over the letter downstairs, she was allowed now little opportunity to make the same mistake with regard to this second one; for a single backward glance from the head of the stairs told her plainly that the object of the old lady's vigilance was now no longer either the one letter or the other—was, instead, herself. Phoebe was following her; and as it chillingly settled upon her that she was totally unable to prevent it, she remembered but too clearly too that, next to her violence, Phoebe's determination had always been the most serious thing about her.

She continued her way downstairs—entered the parlour—left it—passed on through the dining room, the music room—and so, for over an hour without pause, through the rooms and corridors of the huge old house. It was not at all consciously a test of the situation in which she found herself—she had no need of that!—it was the only thing she could think of to do. But when she at last returned, tired, excited, afraid, to her bedroom and to Emma, she couldn't fail to see that it had nevertheless constituted a test indeed. She had scarcely reached her bedside before Phoebe appeared, heavily patient and intent, in the doorway. . . .

Lucia of course knew well enough that it had already shown itself, for Phoebe, a remarkable patience, and knew too that she had nothing to thank for its continuance but Phoebe's uncertainty as to her intentions—that her old sister's steadily deepening suspicion, whose confirmation might result in Heaven knew what, yet remained a suspicion. She didn't underrate the advantage of this—the need for hurry if she were to profit by it. Her difficulty was to snatch, as early as she possibly could, an hour's privacy—and she snatched it at last, during the afternoon, by suddenly leaving the house.

Next day she was constantly under Phoebe's eye, constantly uncomfortable in consequence, and constantly careful to appear as if nothing had happened. She had awakened to find the old lady at her bedside, waiting—had, after the first startled minute, looked closely into her face to read, if possible, what Phoebe knew. What she read was merely that the doubt of yesterday had deepened—and had darkened. For the moment, and for the rest of the day, she counted herself fortunate indeed to have read nothing worse; but it none the less steadily grew upon her that before long she must inevitably be called upon to clear that doubt. Of just how she should do it—of what means, what courage, what subterfuge, what frankness it would require—she hadn't the least clear notion; nothing, indeed, seemed clear now but her persistent disquieting recollection that the lesson of the old lady's desires and determinations had always been that it was as futile to evade as it was dangerous to resist them.

She went nevertheless as usual into the parlour that night, resigned to whatever the next few hours might hold for her, and taking what scant comfort she could from the conviction that whatever happened would doubtless take but a short time. It was well over an hour before anything happened at all—except only that she knitted and Phoebe watched her and waited. It began by being easy enough, in comparison with what it might have been, for Lucia to wait too; but towards the last the stillness, broken only by the clock and the faint click of her needles, grew too long, too tense; and the sharp nervous attention of Milly, the uncertainty of Emma's affected calm, the unwavering inquiring darkening stare of Phoebe, became unbearable. Lucia laid aside her work, met the stare, and confessed—"I've told them not to come."

It seemed to take seconds—minutes—for Phoebe to understand; and she meanwhile merely changelessly stared. But at last, as with surprise, her eyes widened, and then, still slowly, narrowed again; and the lines of her cheek and jaw tightened, her lower lip gradually horribly protruded, her whole head, hideous with rising wrath, thrust forward, and she began to rise from her chair. Lucia got to her feet—stood like the victim of a dream, unable to move, to speak, to think. . . . Phoebe was up—her face, her lifted hands, her whole great figure violently atremble; and while Lucia stood, cold and rigid as a woman of ice, breathless, terrified, Phoebe advanced towards her.

But she had scarce come half way when suddenly, as on that other night, there came a change: Phoebe paused, wavered; the tension dropped; the high constraining charge of everything that had so tremendously prevailed but a second since weakened and passed away— displaced by a stream of music. That it was superb music, that it came from hands skilled to perfection and playing upon their own piano, were details of no importance; what was important was that, as it flowed in upon them, filling the room—filling, it almost seemed, the universe— with its grandeur and its command, Phoebe forgot her purpose. . . .

The first to move was Lucia, widening the space between them— passing, around the table, to a place near Emma. Here, trembling in her relaxation, she watched Phoebe—watched her irresistible surrender to this bondage of beauty against which her purposes, her passions, her will, were as mists in a wind. But if Lucia's eyes, and Emma's, and Milly's, were all for Phoebe, Phoebe had no glance for them. She listened—listened with an intentness which was itself a passion, and at last slowly—it seemed unknowingly—passed to the door, and turned from its threshold in the direction of the music room.

IV

Until her return, four nights later, there was, again, a period of peace; and Lucia, her conscience clear on the point of her duty to the children, and closing her thoughts to everything else—to the unanswerable question, even, of what Phoebe's return might bring—surrendered herself to this interim of intimacy to enjoy it, while she could, at its best. Its result, for whatever reasons of resignation, of hopelessness, of eagerness, of unnamable fitness of mood and circumstance, was remarkably, beautifully successful—was but wonderfully to broaden and to fill as never before her view of the charm and wonder of her privilege—was simply, for the brief delightful period, supreme. . . . But then, to that high and gentle happiness, the contrast at last produced by the reappearance of Phoebe was suddenly, decisively, ruinous.

Its fatal momentary chill was, moreover, not its whole—not its worst—effect. Lucia had still the courage and the ingenuity to have accomplished some small rectification of stolen minutes of escape, of an occasional hour of remote isolation with Emma—provided, of course, Phoebe could but have been kept from suspecting. But even in the first minute of the old lady's renewed presence, as Lucia looked with unquiet inquiry into her face, the conviction dawned for her that the privacy and the pleasure of her beloved comradeship were doomed—that Phoebe knew well enough what her return had done—knew quite to a sufficient degree what the companionship of the twins meant to this one who had opposed her—and knew in consequence what it would cost her to lose it.

The twins had been seated, when she appeared, on opposite sides of the parlour fire, and Lucia had risen to meet her—had matched, for as long as she could stand it, Phoebe's gaze with her own—had finally, at the end of a strained, frightened silence, resumed her chair. Her first concern had been, naturally enough, for what her old sister might do, and it was a relief indeed to conclude at last that she intended to do nothing—nothing, at any rate, but perhaps to take, as usual, her own chair. Phoebe didn't however take her own chair, nor any other; instead, she stepped, and stood, between those of the twins. Lucia, after a first sidelong glance which showed only that she could no longer see Emma, remained seated—waiting, with growing disquiet, to see what would happen. Nothing happened until, at the end of twenty minutes, she looked up. Phoebe's eyes, steady and incurious, were upon her—and so, she supposed, they remained until yet later when, disturbed and offended, unable to stay any longer, she went off to bed.

If Phoebe followed her she didn't know it; she was too vexed, too disappointed, to care. But no degree of vexation could conceal from her the dark old presence next morning, at her bedside—nor could it later, after breakfast, in the parlour, in the halls, in her bedroom—wherever she went to escape it. She soon, indeed, gave up hope of escaping it: it was beside or behind her constantly; and whenever Emma was present it interposed itself, with an intention not so much rude as plainly cruel, between them. Lucia put up with it, all this day and the next and the next, simply because she could do nothing else. . . .

There had been, meanwhile, no uttered communication between them—the signification of look and gesture and movement had been so far sufficient! But on the third night Phoebe, with shattering harshness upon the stillness of the parlour, ended their silence—"You know, of course, that your servants think you're insane!"

After the first startled instant Lucia looked into the passionless watching old face with eyes that scarcely saw—and across her own features marched in quick succession uncertainty, a ripple of amusement, surprise, doubt, unbelief, pain. She looked at Emma, at Milly—and read in their faces all she could have asked of tender, eager sympathy—but nothing at all of refutation for the message of Phoebe. Her eyes dropped then—looked for a long unseeing minute at her empty, limply folded hands—and at last came back to meet again the expressionless gaze of Phoebe—"Really—I don't believe I care very much what my servants think."

But this, though it tried to be brave and calm, was merely weak; and if Phoebe made no answer it might very well have been because she considered none necessary—perhaps considered it enough for the moment to have launched in her sister's mind this notion which, surely, could hardly fail yet further to trouble her.

Whether or not she knew the degree in which she had accomplished just that—knew the depth to which, before another night, this idea that was like an acid had distressingly gone with Lucia—Phoebe waited two days to improve upon her success. Her method then was simply to substantiate her statement by a recital of the servants' reasons for their opinion—those mirrors, this frequent speech for someone they couldn't see, these unearthly hours, the completeness of Lucia's detachment from the normal concerns of her life, this care for the positions of chairs in which she never sat, the frequency with which her thoughts wandered from her work, her food, her conversation. . . . It amounted, for Phoebe, to a fairly long utterance, but it was none the less effective for that; and Lucia didn't attempt to answer it—not so much because most of it was unanswerable, but because she simply lacked heart for the contention that an answer must inevitably have provoked.

As before, Phoebe didn't at once press her advantage—was evidently willing to accept as enough for the moment the pained embarrassment, almost the shame, with which Lucia had accepted this review; but the days following were to show only too well that the old lady was by no means yet satisfied. The next morning brought a deliberate repetition, before Lucia had finished dressing, of the whole unhappy list of her oddities; and by the following night she found it being all but brutally supplemented and expanded—had become the target of taunts of a dozen cruel kinds—about her uncertain health, about her courage, her care for the children, her tenderness for Emma, her personal carelessness, even down to a neglected spot upon her dress. . . .

If Lucia had found it impossible at first to answer her—to say, in fact, anything at all—she found it henceforth sometimes extremely hard to keep silent—to keep from screaming out some desperate defiant answer—to resist flying into this cold impassive face with her fists, her fingers, her nails. But Phoebe, facing her as calmly in that mood as in any other, continued relentlessly her abuse—found fault with half the things she did—harped endlessly upon her eccentricities—made a subject for contempt of anything and everything that marked the Lucia of this time as different from the Lucia of the old—and seemed almost satisfied, even temporarily pleased, when at last, distracted, Lucia frankly fled from her—to spend henceforth as much time as she could out of doors.

But escape even here was not complete, for, from the snow-covered walks of the grounds, she could see the constant dark old figure following her from window to window across the front of the house, watching;

and when the cold grew unbearable and she stole in at the back to seek the kitchen fire, it would be but a few minutes at most until Phoebe would appear in the houseward doorway to await her next move.

It proved at last too much: the deep unrelieved depression of her spirits, the sorrow of this second loss of Emma, the distraction of Phoebe's treatment, the lack of rest, the exposure, amounted to more, all at once, than she could bear. Something gave way—and she awoke one afternoon to find herself looking into the face of a physician.

He was saying something—something not very clear—about her being better—about the time it would take to recover her strength. . . . But she went to sleep again; and only afterward, from her house-keeper—who, a little strangely she thought, was dressed in a nurse's uniform—did she learn how long her illness had already been. . . . And even as she listened she forgot to listen, and her eyes swept the room in search of Phoebe.

Phoebe was not there, nor did she appear until, late in the next month, and with the patient's convalescence assured, the nurse had already for some time left her unattended at night. She awoke then suddenly one morning about three o'clock to see the old figure looming large and dark in the dimness at the foot of her bed, gazing steadily at her. For an instant—long enough for a single chilling start—she was frightened; but then in another moment, suddenly and unaccountably, she wasn't. She looked at Phoebe, oddly at ease, and waited. There seemed to be nothing to say—nothing to do but wait for whatever Phoebe might have to say. And that turned out after a time to be, in substance, sufficiently simple—though the manner of its utterance was hardly usual. It was, from Phoebe, too quiet—seemed quite to justify, in Lucia, her own calmness—suggested, remarkably, that her old sister intended not to be harsh!—"You nearly died."

Lucia didn't answer. Whatever Phoebe's objective—for she must of course definitely have one—it was evidently not, this time, to torment her; and with the comfort of that assurance she could confidently enough—even a little loftily—wait for Phoebe to make herself clear. After a silence Phoebe did—"I don't want you to die."

The manner of her utterance was still quiet enough, but it was still also as free of any shade of warmth or affection as it could well have been; and Lucia found an answer for it which, for dispassionate coldness, all but matched it—"It would have been almost a welcome alternative—to the conditions under which I was living."

Phoebe shrugged—"They were your own choice—the conditions."

Lucia had for a minute to weigh this—had even to verify her interpretation of it—"You mean by that that your actions were my own fault—were my punishment for not doing as you wished about that letter."

Phoebe's confirmation was complete and short—"Of course!" And then after a pause—"You may still choose."

Lucia, thinking it over, deliberately straightening and arranging its elements, again kept her waiting. Then—"I see: if I ask those children to come here—write another letter—get them, for your murderous purposes, into this house—I may have Emma again, as I want her." Pausing here just long enough to be sure of the acquiescence in Phoebe's face, she went quietly on—"And if I don't—if I prevent their coming—you will continue to keep Emma away from me, and torment me for the rest of my life as well. Is that your bargain?"

"Yes." She seemed pleased, as pleased as Phoebe could seem, that their understanding was so far complete; but she wanted it, evidently, perfect—"And, either way, I'll help you to live—for a long time."

Of that, however, the clear conviction of Lucia's reply seemed to make little—"Without Emma though—even with your help—I simply shan't live very long."

Whether Phoebe had an answer for this she never knew, for now quite suddenly her attention was filled with something else—with a vague importunate sense of the presence between them, all about them, of a difference: it pressed upon her as from outside, as though the enveloping shadowed stillness were somehow now otherwise importantly peopled; and as her sense of it deepened she saw, Phoebe's eyes seek the door, saw her face lose its confidence—and looking aside Lucia saw, standing just within the threshold, the stately figure of Katherine.

For a brief still moment she seemed to catch an inward whisper, faint as the echo of a memory, that this was somehow strange. Then, in the scene's strong promise of some higher importance, that surprise, that small pulse of wonder, were quenched; and raising herself upright she waited, without welcome, with only a keen and rising interest, for whatever it might be that this new visitant considered of consequence enough to bring thus for delivery.

What she had brought was but a quiet question, and for Lucia; but its suggestion, from Katherine, seemed of the last strangeness— "Wouldn't it be better—for your own sake—to do as she asks?"

Lucia looked at her long and wonderingly before answering; but then at last, if she didn't understand Mary's mother's attitude, she at least sufficiently understood her own—"I'm afraid—afraid, I mean, for the children."

The rejoinder was ever so gently insistent—"But you have yourself, your own comfort—"

Lucia, shaking her head, interrupted—"My comfort is hardly so important, when I know . . ." She abruptly, curiously, changed her subject—and hardly less her emphasis—"But I don't understand your considering me before them—you of all people!" Then, with sudden narrow-eyed acuteness—"Is it because you think there's no danger for them—because you think you could protect them?"

Katherine didn't for the moment respond; and as she waited Lucia noticed another change, noticed that something—some vague contention—was in process about her in which she oddly had no part, to which she was but a faintly comprehending witness. Her look, following that of Katherine, returned to Phoebe—came back—returned again—watched, fascinated, the action of the influence of the tall commanding figure at her bedside upon the darkly defiant one at its foot. Neither of them appeared any longer aware of her; their eyes, their attentions, their purposes, were wholly for each other. . . . For some minutes—minutes during which, for poor Lucia, the tension heightened to an all but unbearable pitch—Katherine made no movement; but then at last Phoebe did, and Lucia then saw that the woman whose wishes had for sixty years been the law, whose purposes often enough the terror, of their house—whose violence it had been impossible to control—whose will knew no resistance—was being driven from the room. Lucia watched her go—slowly, indirectly, showing her magnificent mistress a face distorted with hate, but going nevertheless. . . .

She disappeared into the shadow of the corridor; the tension dropped; and then, from Katherine, came the answer to Lucia's question—"I could much more easily, should you still not write to them, protect *you.*"

Though this had come unexpectedly, and while her eyes were still fixed upon the black rectangle of her doorway, her mind upon the defeated Phoebe, Lucia detected in it, she thought, the faint falseness of an evasion. Turning, she faced Katherine squarely—"That, you know, I could not ask of you; my problem is my own affair. But the children's is to some extent yours too. . . ." Her voice softened a little—"Please be honest. You don't deny the danger of their coming here; if you admit it why do you want them?—why ask me to write?"

Katherine looked at her closely—even, Lucia thought, a little sadly—"It isn't that I want them here. But your writing would insure you a short period, at least, of peace. You are entitled to that."

"Not at that cost—not at their expense!" This was staunch—was almost stubborn; and Katherine seemed to see that some other persuasion was needed. But she seemed too to wish it had not been—to regret the necessity for explanation—"My purpose in coming here was to help you—to urge you to escape this unhappy, futile trouble. If you cannot accept my protection, I assure you it would be better for you to write. You may trust my concern in the children to be at least as great as your own. . . . What I suggest involves no risk—no greater risk—to them."

The manner of this, the straight persuasive truth of it, left Lucia sufficiently convinced, but left her also still uninformed and wondering—left her, after a silence, but one answer to make—"What you mean then is either that there is no danger, or that it makes no difference whether I write or not." And, as they looked steadily at each other and Katherine didn't answer, she continued—"That's it, isn't it? My not writing again won't prevent their coming!" And even yet, though the deduction was her own, she accepted it with difficulty—"*Is* that what you mean?—that they'll come anyway—in spite, even, of my having asked them not to?"

The change in Katherine's face was confirmation enough—the slightest, most fleeting loss of composure, the faintest trace of what, in another face, would have been a look of desperation—"In spite, I'm afraid, of anything you can do."

V

It occurred to Lucia afterwards that from Katherine's viewpoint her visitation must seem to have come very near to failure; for if, as she had said, its purpose had been to point, for Lucia, a way to relief, she must have seen that the fatal presage with which it had ended must definitely, finally, have precluded the prospect of any relief whatever. But this interpretation—of the visit having failed, simply, of its intention—did not at last satisfy her as complete. There had been in her visitant's face at the moment of her pronouncement that look of discouragement, of half-desperate helplessness; but there had been too, a second later, something else—an extraordinary intentness for Lucia's answering reaction—a sharpness which searched her face—and which seemed to change, from instant to instant, to a look of something like hope. It had been faint enough, but for Lucia it had seemed unmistakable—and seemed moreover, as she subsequently interpreted it, extremely important. . . . For mightn't it be taken—taken seriously—as all the evidence one needed that Katherine's view *had,* in that moment, hopefully changed? Didn't it indeed simply mean that, having come to dissuade a sick antagonistic old lady from an unhappy and futile course, she had discovered in that lady's obduracy a reason to hope that something might yet, between them, be done to prevent the thing she couldn't herself possibly prevent? Lucia ended by thinking so—and by seeing, for Katherine, that Mary's mother might well, at such a time, grasp at straws—that in any case, however faint that unforeseen hope might have been, it must yet, if she admitted it at all, inevitably have defeated the simple and kindly first purpose of her coming.

Their exchange had, at all events, left Lucia an altered view of their problem. It was a darker view, for one thing, than it had yet been; it seemed, for another, to show her that an alliance with Katherine—that any slightest promise of aid from any source whatever—was not, at such a time, to be despised; and its first consequence was that she accepted the alliance. . . . Their understanding, consummated in her first full night downstairs, was briskly stated and without sentiment—"I shall certainly," said Lucia, "do whatever I can . . . and it will help, of course, if you will keep Phoebe away—as you suggested."

She turned then at once to Emma, and they went over the case, seriously, after the manner of their old time, in the fullest detail they could—and, reviewing, analyzing, searching every item and point of doubt, they stopped suddenly to wonder about their sister-in-law's seeming certainty as to the children's coming. It hadn't occurred to Lucia before, nor did it now, to question Katherine's conviction; but it did seem odd certainly that she should be so sure—seemed especially odd, they thought, in view of Phoebe's evident ignorance of it. They were still trying to explain this—still had it prominently between them—when Lucia was startled to discover that their conversation was not, after all, wholly their own—that Milly was there—"Why, don't you *know?*"

The twins, for one silent minute, could but look at her—the old squirming, palely smiling Milly—bursting with a bit of gossip—half afraid to offer it.

"No," at last confessed Lucia, "we don't know. Do you?"

Milly let them have it—"That new woman—your housekeeper—has written; and Mary's mother knows it."

The twins' eyes met, and in their long astounded stare, as Lucia measured the prospect of what a complication *this* amounted to, she felt her purpose sink with discouragement. But she could yet a little sharply question Milly—"Do you know anything more about their communication—Mary's with my housekeeper? How long has it been going on?"

"Ever since she came, I think. I think Mary arranged for her to come here—through the Doctor, you know, before he died. You know, she's no mere housekeeper. . . ." Milly paused—paused deliberately, as if to prolong, to enjoy for as long as she could, for as much as it could possibly be worth, this little moment of importance—as if she were afraid that to hurry might be to lose a little the delight of their interest, their unconcealed eagerness for what she had to tell them. And then as she went on she seemed remarkably more and more to share their attention—seemed to listen to her own statements with a fascination quite the equal of theirs—and seemed not a whit less withal to enjoy the sensation of making them—"It was on a suggestion of hers—something about your condition—that Mary decided to come."

Lucia, a little uncertainly, interposed—"My condition? What do you mean by that?"

Milly hesitated. "I didn't see her letter; I only saw Mary's answer. But it must have been something like—like what Phoebe told you—about what the servants think."

Lucia had now no answer—only a slow, offended flush, as she glanced first at Emma and then away from both of them. But, for the shadow of pain in her own face, there was only the deepest pity for her in theirs. "When," she at last asked, "are they to arrive here?"

And this surely, for Milly, was the triumphant touch: "Tomorrow—that is,"—she glanced at the clock; it was past midnight—"late *to-day*. And nobody else knows that—not even Katherine!"

All but trembling with excitement now, the little woman edged forward, leaned across the table, thrust her queer little face near to theirs—as though, at closer range, to measure more fully the effect of her communication—to taste it at its best—to lose no single shade or suggestion of the joy of it. And when she had watched the passage across their faces—she watched, especially, Lucia's face—of incredulity, of doubt, of consternation—she pushed her pleasure to its peak—"What do you intend to do?"

Lucia rose—"There's but one thing to do. I'll meet them—head them off."

*   *   *

She was accompanied, during the next hour, constantly by Emma—to the attic for a carpet bag, to her bathroom for a tooth brush, to her closet for clothing, to her dresser for handkerchiefs, for hairpins. . . . Although nothing, in this time, passed between them, Lucia had been conscious more than once of a trembling nearness, in Emma, to some utterance; and at last, as she hesitated, bewildered, before a pile of clothing upon her bed, and Lucia stood pensively a little apart, it came out—"Do you intend to come back?"

Lucia shook her head—"I'm afraid they'd come too—afraid they'd follow me."

Emma's response was slow, but when it came Lucia's attention left her packing, left everything, for the surest grasp it could take of the suggestion of this reply and of this half-questioning face—"Wouldn't it be better then, while you can, to prevent their coming back—ever?"

Always, and especially in moments of high feeling, it had been a feature of the similarity of these women that they needed few words for each other; so now it seemed as natural as it was convenient that they needed none—that Lucia's answer could mark their having come, by mere mutual understanding, a great way indeed—"I'd thought of that . . . it seems a terrible thing to do."

"It's the only really safe thing to do, for Dicky—for them all."

Lucia still demurred—"Those people downstairs—the servants—are a difficulty. . . ."

But Emma could meet that: the housekeeper and cook had planned a marketing expedition for six o'clock; the others had remote outside rooms. . . .

There was, then, but one more point—"I haven't planned for it. . . . It would never do, you know, to fail."

But evidently Emma had planned—"You needn't fail. I'll show you."

By dawn Lucia was tired—tired enough almost not to care, as she stood watching at her window, whether her housekeeper and cook went out or not. She was dressed now for the street, and her bag was filled and locked; there was but one thing left to do. But the prospect of doing it—of going again through all those rooms, the attic, the cellar. . . . Her house had never, never seemed so vast . . . !

But then, as she saw on the walk below the two hurrying women, followed by poor ancient Otis with the baskets, she turned resolutely enough to her task. She carried candles and a box of matches; and Emma, constant and eager, followed her.

They went first to the cellar; and as she turned, on leaving it, to see the few small fires already lifting high among the costly kindling of which she had made them, a half-sane enthusiasm seized her for the perfection of Emma's plan. But she saw too, a little fearfully, that if her effort were to realize that perfection she must hurry—prodigiously hurry. The plan was now to dispose of three of the larger inside lower rooms—the library, the dining room, the music room; then three rooms each at the ends of the upstairs corridor; then the attic; then, descending, as many of the remaining second storey rooms as she safely could; and last, on her way out, the downstairs parlour and the great wooden staircase.

She moved swiftly—not waiting to watch, in the dining room, the quick ignition and spread of the flames from chairs and table to panelled wall, nor, in the library, from chair to desk, from shelf to curtained casement. But, approaching the heavy portières of the music room, Emma stopped her—made her listen. It was but a moment's pause, that she might hear, faint, fluent, unmistakable, the sound of the piano— that she might see, among the curtains, the outline of a figure— Phoebe's figure—in fascinated attention for something within the room. The twins exchanged a swift decisive glance and moved on: the music room could wait.

They fairly flew now—Lucia leading, Emma, silent, anxious, urgent, constantly at her elbow—to the second storey corridor. Milly's room with its flimsy furnishings that had never been removed took fire in an instant—though in one of its two selected neighbours she was less— dangerously less—fortunate. Then, as she made for the nursery, pursued by the odor of smoke, impelled now by a mounting fear, she noticed the trailing figure of Milly. . . .

The nursery, full of toys, of wooden cupboards, of clean unpainted furniture, offered no trouble; nor did her own room; of the last of this group, a small store-room next to Phoebe's, she had not time to judge. In the attic, on the hurried advice of Emma, she made but three of the five lightings they had planned, and returned, exhausted, trembling, sick, to the second floor. Here, before the sinister evidence of her success, she saw that there was time for nothing more; only the parlour near the center of the house. . . . She mustn't miss that!

She didn't; but as she turned to leave it—turned with eyes smarting from the sharp pungency of smoke, with skin drawing beneath the heat, with ears full of the faint hum of flames, the crack of burning wood, the dull distant thud of things falling—she came face to face with Phoebe.

For a second, before what she saw in this face of hatred, of chagrin, of towering blind fury, she stood shocked, terrified, paralysed; and then with a cry she turned—turned to run for the greatest distance, some twenty steps, that the room offered. This brought her helplessly, sickeningly, into a corner—where she could do nothing but turn again, cold with terror, to watch the approach of that figure. It came slowly, huge and bent, its hands raised, its distorted face outthrust—horrible . . . hideous. . . . Lucia looked for Katherine—looked into the wide clear hallway down which, if Katherine could but save her from this—for but three seconds—she could yet escape. . . .

She looked again towards Phoebe. And Phoebe had paused, had straightened, had dropped her hands, had now an altered intention— "I'll let you burn!"

Even in her terror, in the heightening physical discomfort of smoke and heat, she could recognize this decision as the choice, simply, of one vengeance before another—the choice, since Phoebe had made it, of the more cruel. But she was to have yet a moment's hope; for suddenly now, like an angel of wrath, Katherine swept into their group—faced Phoebe. Lucia stepped forward, anticipating the instant when this intercession should free her. But she had yet to wait: Phoebe, grimly determined, ignored Katherine, avoided her look, would not, for once, oppose her—but watched Lucia instead, and held her powerless where she stood.

For a second—three, five, ten seconds—she didn't, couldn't, move, and meanwhile Katherine stepped between them, strove to shake, to command, Phoebe's attention. And at last Lucia, seeing the failure of that effort, tried in desperation to escape in spite of it—tried to pass her, tried to circle her, tried even to reach a window—only to be intercepted, turned aside, forced back, by that dark impassable face and figure.

And inevitably at last she saw that it was too late—that her path, the open hallway, was closed. And at the instant of her recognition it seemed also to strike the others—so that as she looked from face to face among them she could but read, in the pity of helpless Milly and Emma, in the grim satisfaction of Phoebe, the confirmation of her own fearful judgment. Katherine, last to face her, last, by a visible decided shift of intention, to admit defeat, approached her—"At least, however, you shall be spared such a death as that."

And now at last—to prevent, clearly, the decisive merciful act that should have stopped Lucia's suffering—Phoebe turned in fierce defiant opposition upon Katherine. And Katherine might in a few minutes have prevailed—for it was now, since Phoebe had met her, but a question of effecting the subjugation she had so often achieved; but Lucia was never to know. For if Katherine was absorbed in that contention, Phoebe was not less so; and even as the tension heightened between those two, the others approached her. Emma led, and there was something strange—something strangely intentional, strangely hesitant, strangely determined, in her face. Lucia saw the white long hands of her sister raised—felt, upon her temples, a gentle touch . . .

*   *   *

Katherine, standing apart, seemed simply to contemplate them— the twins looking, with expressions as of recognition after a long separation, into each other's face; Milly a little shyly watching them; Phoebe gazing darkly, bitterly, upon a grey-clad body upon the floor. Katherine turned away, passed out into the hallway. There was nothing left to do. The reunion of the sisters was now indeed complete.